# Begin
# to Exit
# Here

# Begin to Exit Here

a novel of the wayward press

## JOHN WELTER

Algonquin Books of Chapel Hill
1992

1 — 6 5 1 6

For Leslie Takahashi, who runs through this book like a river.

Published by
Algonquin Books of Chapel Hill
Post Office Box 2225
Chapel Hill, North Carolina 27514-2225

a division of
Workman Publishing Company, Inc.
708 Broadway
New York, New York 10003

Chapter one of this book was first published on the editorial page of the *Kansas City Star,* as a literary sketch.

LIBRARY OF CONGRESS
CATALOGING-IN-PUBLICATION DATA
Welter, John, 1951–
   Begin to exit here : a novel of the
   wayward press / by John Welter.
      p.   cm.
   ISBN 0-945575-51-3
   I. Title.
   PS3573.E4963B44   1991
   813′.54—dc20            91-20295
                              CIP

10   9   8   7   6   5   4   3   2   1
FIRST EDITION

# 1

A woman I was introduced to at a dinner party told me how she buried the wrong dead cat. This doesn't mean she was looking for the right dead cat. She wasn't hoping for a dead cat at all. But seeing a dead cat that looked exactly like hers, one that was exactly the same color and had precisely the same markings as her cat, she picked up the dead cat from the side of the road near her home and cried, knowing she'd never get to see her cat play again, or hold it. And after she found a spot for a funeral and dug up some damp earth, putting her cat down into the ground and crying again, she went very sadly home where no one could soothe her or end her pain. That's when she saw her cat sitting on a windowsill in the living room, staring at her disinterestedly, the way cats do.

1

The woman smiled during that part of the story.

"You mean your cat was alive all along, and you buried someone else's cat?" another woman at the party said.

She smiled and nodded her head.

"At least you buried a dead one. Some people aren't that discriminating," I said.

"Yes," the woman said.

None of us in the little audience had ever heard a true story like that before, and we sort of automatically tried to think of similarly weird and emotional things that had happened to us.

"I buried my little brother one time," I said, lighting a cigarette and then sipping some Royal Crown Cola.

"Kurt, that's grotesque," this woman I know said.

"It was ineffective, too. Mom and Dad made me dig him up. It was on the beach at the Gulf of Mexico near Freeport, Texas. We were playing Crab, which means we squatted along the sand and walked sideways with our hands held out like pincers. The crabs lived in little holes in the sand, and after a while I decided we needed some new realism in our game, so I looked at my brother and said 'I have to bury you, like a crab.' He said okay, or he said something, and then he lay down on his back and I started shoveling wet sand on him with my hands."

"Did you bury him completely?" some guy said.

"No. I had his legs, arms, and torso covered when I realized he couldn't breathe if I put sand over his head, so

I said, 'I can't bury you all the way or you'll die.' He said okay. I think it was the only word he knew."

"I buried my sister in the snow one day," a woman said. "It was in Cleveland and we had a huge snowfall and when my sister and I went out to play in these magnificent snowdrifts, I had her get down on her hands and knees and just covered her completely with snow. I left an opening near her face where she could look out."

"And then did you leave and continue your education and get married?" a woman asked.

"I've never been married," she said.

"What about your sister?" someone said.

"She's never been married, either," the woman said.

"That's not so bad," the woman who buried the wrong dead cat said. "More and more women are postponing marriage."

"It's hard to find a suitable mate when you're buried in snow," I said.

"First we were talking about dead cats. I don't see why we have to get morbid and talk about marriage," a woman said, making everyone laugh.

"I guess we're all at the age where everything starts going wrong," this woman said.

"What age is that?" a woman asked.

"Anything right after birth," I said, enjoying the conversation as it flowed like a flash flood, swamping us all and killing no one.

# 2

The dinner party was held at a house in the relentless woods that inundate nearly all of North Carolina, a state so crowded with trees that children in the public schools have to be shown movies of the sky or they'd never see it. We were at Annie Strother's house north of St. Beaujolais in an area known colloquially as Hoot Owl Hill, which, based on my empirical studies, didn't seem to have any owls, just hills.

"Where are the owls?" asked Janice, the woman who buried the wrong cat. She was sitting next to me on the wooden steps at the bottom of the patio, where we looked off at the thick black outlines of trees crushed together in rural disorder.

4

"They don't have any," I said, cupping my hands over my eyes like binoculars in the garish moonlight as I scanned the treelines. "I've been here lots and I've never seen a single owl."

"A single owl? You mean an unmarried owl?" she said, sipping a glass of something that was probably wine.

"Yes. I've seen married owls, and some divorced ones. I'm doing a film for National Geographic. It's called *Sex on a Swaying Limb*. Actually, I've been here probably a few dozen times, here on Hoot Owl Hill, and I've never seen an owl. Also, I've never heard one hoot. A few times, when I was here for dinner or something, Annie and I'd be out on the patio talking and we'd hear some distant bird going hoo, hoo-hoo, hoo, which I always assumed was a barred owl, or maybe a great horned owl, since I didn't know anything and it didn't matter which owl I assumed it was. Then one day I found out it wasn't an owl at all. It was just a goddamn mourning dove."

"A goddamn mourning dove?" Janice asked, smiling at me with a little of the porchlight shining on her cheek.

"That's the particular variety," I said. "I looked it up in an *Encyclopedia Britannica* for authenticity. There are common mourning doves, and the ones we have out here that annoy me, birds known as goddamn mourning doves. Whenever I hear them now, I yell, 'Quit mourning! It irritates me.'"

"Are you a naturalist?" she said, and pulled out one

of those extremely skinny cigarettes that women are supposed to smoke if they want to look like fashionable militant feminists who wouldn't do anything stupid like smoke a man's cigarette.

"A naturalist? No. A true naturalist wouldn't insult birds like I do. I just like owls. If I was an animal, I'd be an owl."

"You *are* an animal," she said, brushing her hair from her eyes and sipping some wine.

"Did someone spread rumors about me?"

"I don't know you well enough to be privy to your rumors. We're *all* animals. I didn't mean you in particular. Why would you be an owl?"

"Owls are so handsome. They're beautiful."

"They're predators," she said. "Is that it? Do you want to eat live prey, such as goddamn mourning doves?"

"I wouldn't eat anything that complains so much," I said, and lit a Camel Light, the kind of cigarette that men smoke when they're particular about which brand gives them cancer and heart disease.

"If *I* were an animal, I think I'd be a dolphin," Janice said. "I'd be playing in the ocean, jumping through the waves and chasing fish."

"You'd get caught in a tuna net," I said. "If you're going to be an animal, you should be one that isn't endangered."

"Like what?"

"A stray dog," I said. Janice spit her wine out and rubbed the back of her hand across her lips as she giggled and choked on her wine. I tapped her back very lightly, as if that would help her quit choking, and said, "I guess you feel pretty comfortable around me if you can do something as intimate as spit wine. I feel as though we're close."

Politely, I looked away, allowing Janice time to suck in some air, clear her lungs, and wipe the rest of the wine from her lips and chin. When she had done that, she smiled at me with embarrassment and said, "I hope you don't think I'm a barbarian."

"My ancestors were Vandals. They sacked Rome and stole North Africa, so watching someone spit a little wine doesn't offend me," I said.

"Are you German? I'm sorry, but I can't remember your name," she said.

"That's okay. I remember it."

# 3

It was almost a full moon, low in the great dark night, with some Clash album playing on the stereo and the high-spirited, unintelligible background blather of voices coming from the patio above us, all sounding distinctly happy in their private lives except for one voice, a single, distressed male voice producing a brief scream as he fell backward over the patio railing into a holly bush.

"Do you think he's okay?" Janice asked.

"He's screaming. It means he's still conscious," I said confidently. "Holly must be an extremely painful bush. It's a good thing he's drunk, so he can't feel the thorns quite as well."

As two or three men ran down the steps by us to go

inspect the shrill drunk in the holly bush, Janice tapped my knee with her finger and said, "You remember your name, but I don't."

"And why should you? You only heard it once. My parents repeated it to me for months and months until *I* remembered it. I'm Kurt Clausen."

"That certainly is German," she said. "I'm Janice Galassi. Italian, I'm told."

"You don't know?"

She smiled at me and said, "We believe what we're told, don't we? My father says he's Italian and I believe him, which apparently makes *me* Italian, somewhat, even though I don't speak Italian and I was born in Fort Dodge, Iowa."

"You're the first person I've ever known who was born in Iowa," I said, and shook her hand, which made her giggle a little. "I've never thought of Iowa as actually having people in it. I've always thought of it as just this huge piece of land that was given borders and a name so you'd know what to call it when you drove through."

"I don't know. I only lived there until I was three. We grew up, our family, in Philadelphia. Where were *you* born?"

"Odessa, Texas."

"Really? You're a Texan. That's neat."

"I'm only *sort* of a Texan, just like I'm only part German and you're apparently Italian," I said, sipping some

Royal Crown Cola and taking a drag from my cigarette. "I was born in Odessa, in West Texas, and spent the first few years of my life in Brazoria, a relentlessly tiny town in East Texas in the swamps."

"You grew up in a swamp?"

"It's less expensive than a house."

"Were your parents poor?"

"Eventually the Texas Game and Wildlife Commission saw us children floating in the swamp and said nongame animals, such as children, weren't allowed in swamps, so my parents had to buy a house."

"What a fascinating lie," Janice said. "I might write that down for my journalism class for a feature story."

"Journalism? The one thing you can't learn in a journalism class is how to write a story. All they teach you how to do is spit up facts in an orderly fashion. Journalism is rehearsed vomiting."

"You seem a little displeased with journalism," Janice said cheerfully, touching her fingertips lightly on my shoulder.

"It's a noble profession, if what you do for the rest of your life doesn't matter."

"I'm sorry. Annie told me to be nice to you," she said, sounding amused and serious at the same time. She patted my knee and said, "Annie told me a little about your troubles at the paper."

"Annie's a real nice woman."

"I know. She didn't give me much detail on what happened at the paper. She said you might tell me about it, if you weren't too furious."

"I was too furious earlier. I'm tired of being too furious. It's exhausting and unhealthy."

"What happened?" she said.

"Oh, this stupid dickhead son of a bitch at work . . ."

"Is that your editor's formal title?" she said.

I shook my head yes. "It's a pretty formal paper. Anyway, Justin, the stupid dickhead son of a bitch, whose skull I'm going to shatter someday if they make it a misdemeanor, is an Old School editor, meaning he believes that nothing that happens in life can be so complex or human or interesting that it can't be made sufficiently dull and sterile by a trained journalist."

"You're still furious. Annie said you were."

"He despises me because I refuse to imitate the Associated Press or the goddamn *New York Times* and write with that same lofty indifference to life and the blessed reverence for indistinguishable sameness, the stupid bastards."

"Yes," Janice said, as if accepting my furiousness. "And then what?"

"And then yesterday at work I had a routine traffic-accident story that's so tediously common I think it's beyond embarrassing that we even *write* them, since most of our readers don't give a shit who got drunk and wrecked their car again, unless it was Ronald Reagan returning home from a gay bar, or something uncommon like that."

"Yes."

"To make the story at least interesting to me, since I was sure no one else was going to be interested in it, I did what I routinely do, which was ignore the entire history of American journalism and write however the hell I wanted. That is, instead of taking the maddeningly stylized approach favored by nearly every newspaper on the continent and writing something like 'Police charged a St. Beaujolais woman with driving under the influence Thursday after the car she was driving knocked over a U.S. Postal Service mailbox, overturned, and threw the woman from the vehicle,' I wrote it differently, using the same facts. I sat at my terminal and wrote something like 'Mail spewed across Jefferson Street and a woman was disgorged from her car after she lost control of the car Thursday, knocked over a U.S. Postal Service mailbox, and inadvertently parked her car upside down, which is illegal.' It's true and factual, two qualities that didn't interest that fidgety bastard who oversees the paper to make sure that nothing of any interest accidentally gets printed. So he and I argued over the story. He called me into his office, held up a printout of the story and angrily said, 'This isn't good journalism.' I said, 'You're right. It's better than that.' This pissed him off. He said, 'I'm not sure I need you on my staff anymore.' I should've been quiet, but I said, 'No, it doesn't take a full staff to bore the public. Am I fired yet?' And I was. He told me to clean out my desk immediately. I said, 'Am I a janitor now? Wow, I've already got a new job.'"

What happened to me seemed funny, but also dangerous, since I knew that within maybe six or eight weeks I'd be broke, with only the slight likelihood that I could find a job before then, and I was quiet.

Janice laughed at my story and then she was quiet, too, looking at me and trying, I think, to care about me.

"What will you do?" she said.

"I don't know," I said. "That's one of the most honest, useful sentences I keep having to say in my life: I don't know." I smiled wryly, or at least I imagined I did, the way I always smile when something hurts me and I can't stop it.

"Do you dance?" Janice said.

"I don't think anyone would hire me to do that. I have a degree in English."

"I'm not recommending a career, dammit," she said. "I like this *song* and I'm asking you to dance." Someone had put on a Beatles album, and "In My Life" was playing.

"Oh," I said. "So instead of being my guidance counselor, you want to dance?"

"Yes."

I said, "Sure. I love this song, too. But let's not dance on the patio where everyone can make fun of us. Let's dance out in the grass, in the dark."

It was a slow song, and it felt pleasant to have a woman touching my back and leaning her chin on my shoulder and innocently rubbing her thighs against mine, the way people in love do, or the way, like us, that strangers touch and don't feel strange anymore. I wondered if I was going to kiss her. Her hands were flat on my back, and then she moved her hand so one fingertip touched the soft flesh between my neck and my shoulder. I tingled ecstatically, and my penis, having remained aloof until now, showed signs of movement. Those were things you couldn't conversationally tell a woman, so I remained quiet. I wondered, though, if something similar was happening to her but she was too civilized to abruptly describe the activities in her panties. You just don't know.

"You're right," she said quietly as we danced. "The sentence 'I don't know' is probably the most honest sentence in history. By the time we're twenty-one, we're supposed to have picked a career or a set of beliefs to last us all of our lives, although I think most people die without having known what the hell they were doing, really, or if they did anything that mattered. I'm thirty-two, and I hate my job, I'm going to night school, in case that matters, I don't have a husband or a boyfriend, and I buried the wrong dead cat. I don't know."

I laughed and rubbed her back, saying, "I don't know, either. We have that in common."

"You mean ignorance?" she said.

"Yes. It's something to share."

She hugged me and laughed. No woman had done that in a long time, and even though it might have just been a minor affection meaning almost nothing, I was happy. I wanted the song to keep playing so we could keep dancing in the dark in the grass, and then she'd kiss me on the lips and press her breasts harder against me and whisper, "Do you want to sleep with me?" and I'd stare in her eyes and say, "No. I want to stay awake with you." But I couldn't tell her that after only knowing her for about twenty minutes. Maybe after an hour. I wanted my life to work with this stranger, somehow.

Then, we didn't know why, there was a tremendously loud roaring from the side of the house. Janice and I pulled away from each other to look. What we saw was a Japanese sports car crashing into the nineteenth-century tobacco-curing shed that Annie was going to turn into her study, but not now. The unidentified Japanese sports car had slammed through the nineteenth-century front door, and the nineteenth-century wall and roof collapsed onto the hood of the silver car.

"Oh my God. Do you think anyone's hurt?" Janice said.

I said, "If not, they will be. I'll crush the son of a bitch. Annie was going to remodel that tobacco shed and turn it into a study."

Annie was at the front of the crowd that ran from the

house to the car sticking out of the dark shed. Between the patio lights and the moonlight, we could see that the roof of the shed had crumpled the hood of the car. A long beam or log of some sort had pierced the windshield on the passenger's side, and I started to feel sick and panicky, thinking someone's head might have been torn off. But only one person, the driver, was in the car. He opened the door, stood weakly beside the car and said, "I think there's been an accident."

Annie stood near the man, waving her arms wildly and saying, "Goddamn you, goddamn you! You destroyed my shed!"

"He's drunk," Janice said to me. "This just makes me sick."

A man next to us in the crowd said, "Is he okay? Should we call an ambulance?"

"Wait till I beat the fuck out of him," I said, pushing people out of my way as I walked up to Annie, who grabbed my wrist tightly. She looked like she was crying and said, "Kurt! Look what the bastard did!"

A woman who knew Annie and who apparently was a friend of the man who ruined the shed walked up to the wobbly man and studied his face and chest for signs of injury, saying, "David. Are you hurt?"

He shook his head. "I think I'm fine," he said.

I slugged him once in the face, knocking him into the side of his car, where he fell down.

"He's apparently injured," I said loudly, wishing he'd get up so I could hit him again.

"You didn't have to hit him," the woman said angrily and sadly. "He's drunk."

"Then I'll wait till he's sober and kick the fuck out of him," I said.

Janice grabbed my arm from behind me. I couldn't see her, but somehow I knew it was her, like I recognized her grasp. I relaxed a little, and from behind me Janice said quietly, "Don't hit him again. Let's just call the police."

"Why? The police won't hit him."

"Kurt. Calm down."

Annie, who didn't seem to know the man who smashed her shed, was talking to him informally.

"Stupid bastard," she said tiredly as the other woman helped the drunken man stand up. Someone had already called the police and eventually a police car, an ambulance, and a tow truck showed up.

A lot of the other people at the party who'd been drinking beer and wine and liquor tried to act conspicuously sober, as if to dissociate themselves from the repugnant drunk, which Janice thought was funny.

"Now we act morally superior to him, even though half of us are drunk, too," she said. "We're, I think, simply drunk at a more respectable level. Except you," she said as we watched the paramedic examine the drunken man on the patio. "I haven't seen you drink any alcohol all night."

"I don't drink," I said.

"Do you do anything at all?" she wondered pleasantly.

I didn't want to tell her yet that I'd quit drinking nearly a gallon of dry sherry a day because I thought I was an alcoholic, so I tried to look indifferent and said, "I inhale aviation fuel."

The paramedic was saying to the drunken man, "You're terribly lucky. A building fell on you and all you have is a bruise on your cheek."

"As soon as we realized he was okay, Kurt slugged him in the face," Annie said. "Can someone hit him again before you take him away?"

The drunken man pointed at me and said, "I want to press charges."

"Why don't I just press your mouth shut?" Annie said.

"Were there any witnesses?" a police officer said. About seventeen people saw me hit the man.

"It was dark," Janice said.

"It still is," someone said.

"It reminds me of night," a voice said.

"Me, too."

The police had no choice but to take the drunken man away, and after the tow truck pulled the sports car from the vanquished tobacco shed, Annie stood next to her boyfriend, Thomas, and studied the crumbled, dark ruin, the splintered, sad-looking timbers. It was perfectly quiet, now, except for a Rolling Stones album screeching respectfully from the house, and everyone waited to see what Annie would do. Staring at the shed, she spoke mournfully, saying, "I don't know. Almost everyone told me after I bought this house that the old tobacco shed was just a stupid, worthless, decaying shed, that it had no architectural or historic value. But I always imagined the people who built it, sawing down pine trees, cutting the logs, struggling everywhere to make every piece fit just right, inventing something out of the wilderness more than a full century ago, leaving it standing here as ordinary evidence of vanished lives."

As I imagined the vanished lives represented by the destroyed shed, I almost started crying.

"I guess we could build a bonfire out of it," Annie said, and that's what we did. People got fallen limbs and branches for kindling from the woods, the endless, maddening woods, and others of us carried and dragged nineteenth-century timbers from the shed to the gravel driveway where the men, like pioneers, constructed a pyramidal stack of wood that kept falling over.

"How do you build a bonfire?" Thomas asked whoever was listening.

"You need some bon," I said. "Janice? Will you ask Annie to go to the store and get some bon?"

"Bon my ass," Annie said with amused impatience.

"Is that a brand name? I guess you go to the store and ask which aisle the bon my ass is on," I said as Annie and

Janice helped the men build an improved pyramidal stack of wood that kept falling over. We decided to just crisscross the timbers and things and use an engineering technique described by Annie when she said, "Just stack the shit. Don't make it pretty. We're going to set it on fire." Three or four people brought out folding aluminum chairs, although most of us just stood in the driveway around the stack of wood, which was about three feet deep and about five feet in diameter. And then, to make it an authentic nineteenth-century–style bonfire, I poured two gallons of gasoline on the wood and lit the fire with a rolled-up sports section of the *New York Times*. There was a minor explosion. People screamed unnecessarily loudly as a few streams of burning debris were flung upward several feet in reddish orange chaos, but most of the debris fell back into the fire, and although one woman and one man complained of minor burns on their arms, the bonfire was widely regarded as a success, driving away the great dark night, or maybe just making it more conspicuous as we stared with pointless fascination at the swirling flames.

# 4

It was the first party I'd been to where we set a building on fire. Not that much in life was particularly rational. A repellent drunk had destroyed Annie's beloved tobacco shed, and after we had him arrested and taken away, people dismembered the shed, set it on fire, and resumed getting appreciably drunk as they chatted and joked and flirted around the burning driveway.

"Are we civilized?" Annie asked in a quiet, slightly curious voice as she stared at everyone standing and walking and sitting along the perimeter of the fire. She sipped German wine from a Dixie cup as she sat cross-legged on the ground behind Thomas, leaning her chin on his shoulder.

"Of course we are. We invaded Panama," I said, drink-

21

ing a bottle of IBC Root Beer and smoking a Camel Light. "No one is regarded as civilized unless they invade somebody. That's history."

Annie smiled at me. "*I* didn't invade Panama," she said.

"I didn't, either. I stayed home that night," I said.

Janice, who sat cross-legged beside me with one of her knees almost touching mine, laughed a little and stared at me. I wanted her to like me. I wanted her to take me home. She was one of the nicest strangers I ever didn't know, and I wished she'd kiss me, was what. How do you find somebody? By accident. You wait for the right accident and someone's there, staring at you.

"I don't think invading a tiny Central American country means you're civilized," Thomas said as he threw a pinecone into the bonfire.

"Yeah. Panama *is* pretty small. We should've invaded Canada," I said.

"You're not supposed to invade your allies," Janice said.

"When I asked if we were civilized," Annie said, "I didn't mean is the United States civilized. I meant are *we* civilized, here? A man drives a Japanese car into my nineteenth-century tobacco shed because he's drunk. And do we settle anything, make the world better? No. We rip the shed apart, pour gas on it, and have an explosion and fire in my driveway."

Janice leaned her head in front of me to look at Annie and say, "At least we had the guy arrested for destroying your property, so we could set it on fire."

I liked her even more. A deep sense of irony in a woman was as important as breasts and a vagina. Again I'd thought of something I couldn't tell her. I realized you usually can't talk about sex, even if you're not having it.

The fire was burning pretty violently, then, with yellowish orange flames whipping against each other, rising about six feet or higher and shooting unpredictable bursts of embers up into the dark, like thousands of tiny red stars escaping into the night. People were sweating. It was already eighty-seven degrees that night, and the bonfire got it up to maybe a hundred and thirty degrees, we guessed, within six feet of the fire.

"This is my favorite southern tradition: Sweating," I said.

"That's not a southern tradition," Annie said.

"I guess it's just a southern misfortune, then."

"Shut up."

"*Fuck* it's hot," Thomas said.

"I always wished the TV weatherman would say that one day," I said.

"I think we should move away from the fire," Annie said. We all got up, backed away, and started walking to the patio to get something cold to drink. Janice asked me what I'd thought of doing, now that I'd been fired from the paper. I told her I might write a southern novel called *As I Lay Sweating*. She said, as she playfully rubbed some sweat from my forehead with her finger, that I couldn't write a southern novel because I wasn't a southerner.

"I know. Maybe I'll write a German novel," I said as we walked up this big hill behind Annie's house, just sort of spontaneously deciding to go up on the hill together, with neither of us saying why, like we didn't know.

"But you're not really German, either," she said.

"No. I'm not really anything. I guess that makes me American."

The light from the bonfire was bright enough for me to see her smiling at me, and I was happy, even though I scarcely knew her and, as far as I knew, this might be the only time I'd ever see her. The world put people together as randomly as it guaranteed that nothing would work and your hopes were stupid. But I kept liking her, in case it would work.

She carried with her a glass of some blush wine or something, and I had a new bottle of IBC Root Beer. Near the top of the hill was a little spot next to the trail that was cleared and padded with thousands of dry pine needles where we sat together and stared down at those idiots, our peers, who apparently had found a pitchfork and were using it to roast hot dogs over the bonfire.

"Look at them," Janice said. "It looks like a cookout in hell."

"I've never seen a cookout in hell, but maybe you're right," I said, watching this tall guy with glasses hold the pitchfork close to the edge of the fire with little dark things impaled on the prongs. We assumed they were hot dogs. Naturally this led to a discussion of theology.

"Do you get to eat hot dogs in hell?" Janice asked.

"The Bible doesn't say. It's badly underwritten."

"Do you believe in hell?"

"No. I think eternal damnation is too long."

"Too long? How long should damnation be?"

"Maybe a month. I think being in a lake of fire for thirty days is long enough."

She looked at me and laughed. "You sound like a heretic," she said. "You could go to hell for not believing in hell, you know."

"I worry about that. Maybe on Judgment Day I'll bring a lawyer with me. You know, stand around with a few billion sinners from all of history, waiting for your turn to be held accountable for every instant of your life, and while everybody else around you is crying and whimpering, waiting to see if their names are written in the Book of Life or not, I'd say, 'Look at me. I brought an attorney. Ha, ha.'"

It made Janice spit wine again and laugh.

"I'm sorry," I said. "In a way, though, I like watching you spit wine. It's either sensual or sensuous. I forget which."

As people down in the yard and the driveway wandered around the bonfire, moving in and out of the light like ghosts in summer clothes, dancing and, I assumed, preparing in some cases to go copulate, Janice and I talked among the pine needles, beginning to know each other. She said she moved here in 1978 to study archaeology at the University at St. Beaujolais.

"Bones?" I said.

"When people die, that's frequently what they become," she said. "But you know what you're more apt to find than bones?"

Of course I didn't, but I at least wanted to guess. "Dirt?" I asked.

"Trash," she said. "The one thing that all ancient and modern cultures produced with universal proficiency was trash. I went into archaeology, my God, with the usual vague dreams of helping discover profoundly interesting and stunning Indian villages and burial sites filled with relics and artifacts and maybe even world-crushing evidence of esoteric religions or fantastic jewels and things."

"Like *Raiders of the Lost Ark*?" I wondered.

"I love that movie, but, archaeologically, it sucks," she said.

"Sucks. You're using academic terms."

"By the time I got my degree in 1982 and spent time at local Indian digs, I realized that much of what we'd ever find in the search for important knowledge of lost cultures was just real old trash, like burned-up animal bones, charred beans, and the general discarded crud from pre-historic dinners."

"Really? And then what did you do? Do you teach?"

"I used to, for a little while, but the pay is so horrible. I could barely afford to live in squalor."

"Ah, squalor. I was probably one of your neighbors."

"Have you lived in squalor?"

"Next door to it. Several times."

"Anyway, where was I?" she asked.

"In squalor. I was your neighbor."

"Yes, yes. And when I kept realizing I'd picked a profession where jobs are extremely hard to find, and when you get one you have a master's degree and the salary of a dishwasher, I finally became something people never heard of. I hate to say it. It sounds so abstract and unreal." She kind of grinned and grimaced at the same time.

"Tell me, tell me," I said, because I didn't care what she was. I liked her, and I'd like anything she told me.

"I'm a statistical research assistant in viral epidemiology," she said.

It took a while to think about such a long title. I patted her leg and said, "John Keats wrote a poem about that: 'Ode on a Statistical Research Assistant in Viral Epidemiology.'"

She thumped my cheek with her finger. "You're a charming lunatic. Annie told me you were. I see no reason to disagree with her."

"That's almost like being complimented, isn't it?"

"Almost."

After I walked down the hill to get some more blush wine and root beer and happily walked back up the hill to sit next to Janice and wonder if she'd undress and pin me to the ground where I wouldn't resist, I looked up at the almost-full moon and kind of contentedly smiled at Janice, saying, "It's pretty exotic sitting with a woman under the summer moon, talking about bones and viral epidemics."

She closed her eyes and laughed. I think we got along spontaneously, or accidentally, or one of those qualities you think you're identifying when really you're just suddenly happy and you don't know why, but you hope it doesn't quit and get replaced with the normal emptiness and sadness of being alive one more day alone.

For a while she talked about having visited Canyon de Chelly in Arizona and looking at the fantastic Indian ruins fastened so solidly and improbably to the canyon wall that it looked, she said, "like the wall grew a home for the Indians. And then you have to imagine, because there are no records, these primitive people without winches or cranes building these monstrous, thick networks of walled homes along the sheer edges of goddamn cliffs. And all the Indians are gone. Vanished. Inexplicably leaving behind an entire city in a canyon so that, one day, our rowdy European ancestors out conquering the continent and smugly stealing whatever the hell they wanted could come along and discover some ruins."

Sipping my root beer in the humid, hot dark, I looked at Janice and said, "My ancestors didn't look for ruins. They made them."

She said, "What?"

"I'm part German. That means I'm descended from the Vandals and Visigoths and Ostrogoths and the regular Goths."

"So? Is that bad?" she said.

"It was back then. They walked around Europe saying, 'Look. A nation. Let's steal it.' Or if they didn't want to steal a country or it was too hard to do at the moment, they'd walk through a city and break it. *Crack. Ha, ha. There goes your civilization.* Do you know what they did one time? While wandering through Europe on a customary rampage, the Vandals sacked Rome. Some people can say of their heritage, and maybe *you* can, since you're part Italian, that they're descended from people who built ancient Rome. All I can say is my ancestors liked Rome so well they robbed it. Jeez."

Janice put her hand on my knee and said, "Don't sack me."

"I don't know you well enough to sack you," I said. "I'm one of the polite Germans. I say, 'May I sack you, please?'"

"You're evidently thinking of an expanded, more personal meaning for sack," she said, smiling ironically.

"At first I wasn't, but I am now," I said, happy and scared and astonished that in a few seconds my discussions

of the plunderings of ancient Germans had been transformed by Janice into a metaphor for sex. I didn't know
what to say. I pretended to be interested again in the people
around the bonfire.

"There's another southern custom I think I like: People roasting marshmallows on a pitchfork over the remains
of a burning shed," I said, looking over at Janice to see if
this latest insidious insight of mine seemed funny and dis-
tracting to her, and if she maybe had a somewhat erotic
look on her face, as if she were thinking of how we might
sack each other. She was smiling, but why I couldn't be
sure.

"I'm starting to get a little drunk," she said, pouring
her wine into the pine needles. "I better drive home while
I still can." And in the same instant when I was sad that
she was going to leave, as if suddenly she was tired of me
and I wasn't at all the kind of man she wanted to know, she
said, "Would you like to go home with me and look at my
artifacts?" And she started laughing, as though I were embarrassed and she found that charming.

I was going to say I'd been looking at her artifacts all
night, but instead I just said, "Yes."

# 5

She lived in a small basement apartment overlooking the core of the Earth, was how she described it to me when we got there. As she gave me a brief tour of her apartment, she said, "These are genuine cinder-block walls, not cheap imitations. Notice how they retain moisture, allowing for the uniform growth of mold and mildew. This apartment is ecologically balanced. I sometimes have spiders, earthworms, crickets, and centipedes, which I really despise and kill as often as I find them. A physics professor I had in college said that if we humans finally destroyed the planet in a nuclear cataclysm, bugs would survive and dominate the Earth. I think they're already trying that in my apartment, so I'm engaged in a guerrilla war to usurp them."

There was a neat old antique desk of some sort in her little living room, made of polished, dented maple with brass handles on the drawers. When I pulled open the center drawer to look at whatever papers and things would be in the neat old desk, there was a big black pistol there next to a loaded magazine stuffed with large bullets.

"Janice?" I said to her in the kitchen, where she was fixing me some Italian coffee and getting some wine for herself. "Do you shoot centipedes with a nine-millimeter semiautomatic Beretta?"

She looked at me through the kitchen doorway and smiled, then started laughing, holding her hands over her face in surprise or embarrassment as if, oh, no, I'd found the silly little nine-millimeter Beretta. I held up the gun and said, "I guess if a bad viral epidemic breaks out, you'd treat patients with this?"

She walked up next to me, still laughing, and put her hand lightly on my back and said, "My father gave me that on my birthday last August."

"A gun? For your birthday?"

"I'm supposed to shoot you if you behave badly in my apartment."

"I don't think I will."

"My father read some newspaper story about date rapes. He got upset and bought me that gun, so I guess if things go badly tonight, I'll have to shoot you in the forehead, if you don't mind."

"Things won't go badly," I said, putting the gun back in the drawer. "How many men have you shot?"

"I don't count them," she said, patting my back and returning to the kitchen, where I followed to be near her and get some coffee.

"Dating is a lot different now than when I grew up," I said. "Men are supposed to carry condoms and women are supposed to carry guns."

"And you men have it a lot easier than women, as usual. Condoms aren't nearly as expensive as guns," she said.

"I wonder," I said, "if the Catholic Church would oppose guns as a form of birth control? If you shoot someone to avoid pregnancy, is that contraception?"

"It's probably manslaughter," Janice said.

She turned on her big ceiling fan with the brass-tipped wooden blades and turned on her little dehumidifier in the corner next to a potted ficus tree decorated with little white Christmas lights, and then she had me sit next to her on the musty but comfortable sofa under the pale light of a beaten-up, antique floor lamp with a huge burgundy shade pleated and rigid as a starched skirt. The desk was at the end of the sofa on my side, so I said, "Do you want to sit on this side? The gun's over here."

She said, "No. You can just hand it to me if I need it."

"Okay."

At first, as the ceiling fan steadily blew humid, cool air

on us and we adjusted to the silent weirdness of sitting
there together at last for our known and unknown reasons
that we hoped were the same, Janice sat cross-legged in her
white shorts and peach-colored sleeveless blouse, leaning
her elbow on the back of the couch, slowly twirling a thick
strand of her dark brown, nearly black hair, looking at me
and smiling a little, as if studying with satisfaction this
strange new man she'd brought home. I wondered how
soon she'd reach for me, or if I'd reach for her first. I just
wanted to hold her. I'd wait.

"Well, are you going to show me your artifacts?" I said,
lighting a cigarette and then sipping some very hot coffee.

She sniggered quietly and grinned. "I'm not sure I
know you well enough to show you my artifacts just yet,"
she said. "Tell me more about how you grew up in a swamp
in Texas and where you went to college and why you're in
North Carolina and if you hope to do anything in life that
matters before you grow dim and vanish, like we all will."

"All that? Jesus Christ, we could be up all night."

"I'm not sleepy."

"Well, you will be when I'm done, if I get done."

"Tell me some stories, Kurt," she said, and stretched
one of her legs out across my knees, and I liked her some
more, wishing she knew that. So then I told her some stories, pretty abbreviated, so she wouldn't fall asleep.

I told her I lived in Texas only long enough to learn
that the beautiful black and red and white coral snakes

didn't want to be picked up because they could kill you. And you shouldn't pet alligators because *they* can kill you. One of the first things I learned as a boy was that I was obviously going to die one day, and maybe pretty soon if we continued living in southeast Texas, which was filled with handsome reptiles that evidently wanted to kill everybody. When I was maybe four or five, my father got some new job in Wichita, Kansas, and so we all drove to Wichita, where eventually I learned that my father was a chemical engineer. He worked for the Air Force doing secret, abstract shit that had something to do with all of those underground missiles in Kansas, the Titan missiles with nuclear warheads. We were the only kids, my big sister and I, that I knew of whose father worked on missiles that could blow the fuck out of the whole world. We knew abstractly, the way little kids do, that it was the Russians who were going to blow *us* up with their hydrogen bombs and nuclear missiles if *we*, the United States, weren't stronger than they were with bigger and more numerous underground missiles and so on, and so it seemed rational and patriotic to have missiles that could kill everyone on the planet, although ultimately it made no goddamn sense at all and just horrified us.

"What's your sister's name?" Janice asked.

"Kristen. We, Kristen and I, had a hideout in the woods near our house, out by a big creek that was dried up most of the time. There were these long rows of big trees that grew along the creek. They were hedge apple trees, meaning they grew this big, useless green fruit with bumps all over it that I don't think any human or animal could eat. They were the size of softballs, and the only use we ever found for them was to throw them at the trees and smash them open. Anyway, the hedge apple trees grew pretty close together, and my sister and I found some old tin from a crumbled farm shed and some other boards and junk out in the fields and used it to build a little hideout with a roof and a door and no windows. And sometimes when we went there with maybe some Hostess Twinkies or some kind of food like that, we'd pretend that the Hostess Twinkies were our provisions during the end of the world, when all of the missiles were flying and the bombs were being dropped and huge, massive mushroom clouds bigger than thunderheads turned the sky orange and gray and black. It was stupid, but we thought that being far enough out in the woods could protect us from nuclear explosions and we wouldn't die. And we'd sit in the dirt in our hideout with the wind blowing in through all the big cracks and through our door, and stare off across the plains and study every cloud changing along the horizon, wondering which one might become a mushroom cloud and start killing us all. One time Kristen started crying. We weren't even talking about anything. She was just rolling a hedge apple in a circle on the dirt, looking out at the big summer sky as a giant thunderhead swelled up a long way off. I think the thunderhead had a rounded top, sort of, and maybe Kristen thought it looked like a mushroom cloud, and her head started trembling a little and she started crying. I held her hand with both of mine, and this is making me real damn sad. I don't think I want to remember this now, or I'll start crying, dammit."

Janice sat up quickly and held my hand. "You can cry if you need to," she said and touched my cheek with her fingertips. "I think you just wandered into your childhood again and remembered something terribly sad. Let's wander into the kitchen. I'll get you some more coffee or a Coke or something, and I promise I won't let the Russians blow you up, okay?"

"Instead, you'll shoot me with your Beretta," I said.

"Maybe not. You're behaving very well. It doesn't appear as if I'm going to have to kill you. I like that."

In the kitchen as I leaned against the oven and watched Janice stooping over to look for things in the refrigerator, I happily stared at the contours of her butt and said, "You know what? You have a wondrous butt."

She turned her head sideways to look at me. "You're not sad anymore," she said.

I shook my head no.

"Thank you for liking my butt. No one's ever called it wondrous before."

"I'm glad to be the first."

She fixed a plate of some kind of French cheese and

rye wafers and poured herself a little more Gallo and poured me a glass of ginger ale, and with that little feast, we went back to the couch where Janice announced, "I like your butt, too."

"Thank you. I'm glad we agree on each other's butts."

Returning to the importunately abbreviated story of my life, I told her that if the Great Plains were going to kill my sister and me, it wouldn't have been a Soviet missile but an ordinary thunderstorm and its lightning, tornadoes, and floods. You could even die from hail. One time in Wichita we saw hail the size of dog heads. Then we wondered which was worse: radioactive fallout or hail as thick as dog skulls? Of course we never knew, and then, because of my father's secretive career in the defense industry, things changed radically, and in 1965 we moved to an elegant and fantastically expensive home in Mission Hills, Kansas. That's a little city that serves as an elite refuge for the upper-middle class, right across the state line from Kansas City. When my father got his new job as a senior staff engineer and we moved into what I thought was our little palace in Mission Hills, I realized that being on the refined verge of worldwide annihilation paid well. I had a bedroom the size of a bowling alley. I'm lying. It was only as big as a church. Kristen and I decided that the huge downstairs fireplace was wide enough and deep enough to put some dirt on the floor and grow firewood. And then you could put in some Indians and bears and deer and have a civilization in the fireplace. But Kristen, who's a year older than me, refused to be awed and content with our thermonuclear wealth, and one day in November, when there was snow everywhere and we were outside, she looked at our big gingerbread house and said something like 'Kurt, this is no better than Wichita. The Russians can still blow us up. They know we're here.'

"I said, 'They know we're in Mission Hills? Who told them?' I was a charming, dumb-ass little boy. And then what, what? And then of course in the following years I began to grow up, become educated, get venereal disease, serve as an acolyte in the Episcopal Church, fall in love, get mangled on my own recognizance, and finally, the really big decision in my formal misdevelopment, go to college to study English, enabling me to remain unemployed for as many consecutive years as I could endure. And here I am, an innocent, thermonuclear white guy in the South. Am I being coherent? I apologize if I am."

# 6

She smiled at me kind of gently, musingly, as if visualizing part of what I'd just told her and wondering, while looking straight into my eyes, if I was the kind of man she wanted to be next to on the couch. It might have been a moment where two people who have been talking for a long time and like each other immensely at last run out of spontaneous things to say and they're left in the big quiet, the place of dumb, anxious existence again where you don't even know why you're in the world or in the room, or whether or not proceeding with your life can happily involve this person you're looking at, or if you should just go away, or what. I wondered if she was sleepy and would ask me to leave, like I had a good place to go to, but I didn't, unless it was her. *She* was the good place. I was afraid to tell her that. Everything was quiet now, and we stared at each other. I was trying to memorize her face, and I badly wanted to kiss her.

"What time is it?" she said, even though she could see from my bare arms that I didn't have a watch.

"Night," I said. "I don't have a watch, so that's only an estimate."

She struggled not to laugh, then laughed loudly, kind of gleefully shaking her head and thumping the bottoms of her bare feet into my thigh.

She straightened herself on the couch, sitting cross-legged with one of her knees now resting on my thigh, and I was happy. She lit one of my Camels and took a sip of wine. "Do you have to be anywhere in the morning?" she said.

I think this meant she was going to ask me to stay, and I was jolted with pleasure and tension. "No," I said.

"I have a small bed," she said, looking into my eyes.

"Mine's not very big, either," I said.

"You're a strange man."

"I know."

"I have a fan in the bedroom, in case it gets too hot."

"So do I. You're a lot like I am."

She smiled and put her hand on my cheek. "Is it time for you to go home?"

"I don't want it to be."

"I have a question."

"What?"

"Would you be upset if I undressed and laid down on you in my bed?"

"I'd be upset if you didn't."

She closed her eyes and I closed mine.

"I can't see you," I said, feeling her breath on my face.

"I'm close," she said, leaning her lips into mine, and a tingling wave of lightness and warmth rushed through me. It wasn't just chemicals and DNA. It was her. She kissed my cheek and my eyelid, and then my lips again, leaning down onto me with her full weight, pressing her breasts against my chest and wrapping her legs around mine. I almost cried from the suddenness of her happening to me. I tried not to, squinting my eyes shut, but she could sense it and lifted her head up in front of my face and said, "What's wrong? You're starting to cry."

"I won't. I'm fine."

"But why would I make you cry? I want you to be happy."

"That's it. I am. Good things don't happen to me, and suddenly, here you are happening to me. I don't know why." I put my finger in my mouth and bit it. She pulled my finger from my mouth and kissed me.

Quietly into my ear, she said, "I *want* to happen to you. That's why I haven't shot you."

I looked in her eyes. "Do I get to see your artifacts now?"

"Better than that," she said. "You get to see me."

# 7

"If you didn't want to be unemployed, you shouldn't have gotten fired," Janice said in her soft, playful voice.

"I know," I said, distractedly watching Phil Donahue on television interviewing a transvestite from the Transvaal.

"Just get in your car and drive out there and see if they'll hire you, Kurt. You can get a good job later. You just need some money from somewhere. Go to the interview. I'll fix you a Chinese dinner tonight, okay?"

"This is ludicrous. I feel stupid."

"Kurt. I know it's weird, it's very weird, but try it. It's a job."

"Okay. Here I go. I'll see you tonight. Wish me luck, or something random and uncontrollable."

43

"Something random and uncontrollable? Lord, you're the most sardonic man I ever knew."

"I guess I have to excel at something."

"You'll be fine. I'll see you tonight."

"Okay. Here I go. Bye-bye."

"Bye."

As I drove out the highway past Small and the endless pine forest crowding up to the edges of the highway like gangs of trees letting me pass by, I tried to think of the stupidest job I ever had. There were too many. At Royals' Stadium in Kansas City, I was the only beer vendor with a degree in English. The other vendors, almost all of them inner-city blacks, made fun of me for being an almost-black because I had a job like theirs.

"I'm part Comanche. Fuck you," I told them sometimes.

"What's Comanche?" they'd say.

"Don't you dumb bastards watch cowboy movies? A Comanche's an Indian. You shouldn't be allowed to be a goddamn beer vendor if you don't know the names of the Indian tribes we stole this country from."

But during the ball games it was occasionally useful to have studied literature, such as when one of the infielders missed a ground ball and I could say to whomever I was pouring a beer for: "He evidently believes a man's reach should exceed his grasp." Or one time when the Royals were playing the Yankees, whom Kansas Citians despised, and the Yankees were ahead by one run in the bottom of the ninth inning and the last Royal struck out, I was able to yell, "Rage, rage, against the dying of the ninth!"

And now everything was ruined again, hopeless and wretched and other appropriate sentiments no one would pay you for knowing, because I was so desperate for work that I was applying to be the toll-free telephone operator at the most amusing and shameful business in Vermilion County: East of Eden Enterprises, a mail-order and catalogue pornography company. I never could be sure why so many people believed that pornography was insidious and evil. The one constant fact of history was copulation. Which reminded me of a good way to enrage people and get in serious trouble. In 1974 when I was a student at Rockwell College in Kansas City, a couple of the more orthodox students there, Catholics, too, were holding a maddeningly pretentious discussion on morality and literature and said *Playboy* magazine shouldn't be regarded in any way as respectable, even if it published stories by Vladimir Nabokov or anyone else, because it was prurient and had photos of genitalia. I had a sudden insight and said, "What's wrong with genitals? Even the pope has those."

It was an unwelcome insight, and although I was irrefutably right, one of the students grabbed me by my shirt and tried to throw me down. He yelled, "You son of a bitch!"

"That's not scripture," I said, and put him in a head-

lock until a Jesuit priest ran up and threatened to expel
us. He asked who started the fight. Unfortunately the student who started the fight was still too angry to be rational,
and he pointed violently at me and said, "He said the pope
has reproductive organs!" Intelligently, the priest groaned
and walked away. Maybe I shouldn't have been in a Catholic school.

The future was unavoidable and soon I was driving
into the parking lot at East of Eden. I wished I still drank,
so I could've had a glass of dry sherry before going in, to
give me that fake peace and equanimity you can get from
a sudden rush of alcohol. But I was starting to believe that
being sober was more interesting, like when you're a kid
and the pure weirdness and wonder of the world swarms
over you undiluted. Inside the building I met the vice president of the company, who I thought looked strange
dressed in a blue business suit at a company that sold videos of naked people licking genitals. The interview was
held privately in a windowless room that I noticed had sam-
ples of pastel rubbers and, on one wall, a Norman Rockwell
calendar. The man looked at my job application and resumé, then, almost smiling, said, "Are you familiar with
our product line and our mass market?"

"Yes. You sell erotic materials," I said, hoping to sound
straightforward and pleasantly terse.

"Correct," he said. "For example, we sell therapeutic
aids approved by marital counselors, such as three-speed
vibrators."

"Wow," I said. "Three speeds. You could get some mileage there."

"Indeed. Are you familiar with any of our catalogues?"

"No, but I have a degree in English. I'm sure I could read them."

"All of our business transactions at East of Eden are conducted with full confidentiality and in accordance with all pertinent federal, state, and local regulations."

"Of course."

"We handle two-hundred to three-hundred phone calls a day from adults ordering primarily color videos of the full range of mature sexual possibilities, excluding any depictions of children, brutality, or domestic animals. We also provide a considerable supply of therapeutic aids used in private practice and national research, such as lifelike Amazon dildos, glow-in-the-dark condoms, portable, vibrating vaginas, and full-size, realistic sex dolls with hair and crack-resistant orifices."

"No one likes cracks," I decided to say.

The vice president almost looked directly at me, aiming his eyes slightly away, as if from modesty, and said, "Do you find any of this obscene?"

"I'd say most of it's obscene, but if the customers don't mind it, you might as well sell it to them."

# 8

Depression and shame leaked into me from the instant I was hired, and I imagined I felt like a whore, except a whore had a vagina and I didn't, which made me say to myself, "See? I can't even be a whore. The lowness of my condition doesn't even have an appropriate name for it." I tried to think of a word, a name, for the kind of person I was who, out of unavoidable desperation, accepted whatever depressing, useless, vile job came along.

"A human," I said. "That's the kind of person I am."

When I got to Janice's apartment that evening, she was slicing some fresh pork to fix us a Chinese dinner.

"Oh boy. More southern food," I said in a joking, very quiet voice.

Janice hugged me and kissed me, leaning her head back and saying, "How'd my boy do today?"

"Things went badly," I said.

"What happened?"

"They hired me."

She smiled a little, gently. "But, Kurt, until another paper or somebody will hire you, you need a job."

"I'll be selling pornography on the phone."

"Maybe I'll call you at work and buy something," she said, grinning at me affectionately. "What do you sell?"

"Movies."

"Like *Snow White*?"

"Not unless Snow White masturbates or something."

"Well. This is a strange job. Do they have any of those sicko bestiality videos?"

"No. They don't sell wildlife videos. I need to go sit down and feel awful for the rest of my life."

After dinner, when I was sitting morosely on the couch, drinking some Coke and smoking a cigarette and watching a documentary on public television about Amazonian piranhas biting each other's fins off because it was easier than finding other fish, Janice put her head on my stomach and stretched out on the couch next to me, making me wonder if she was going to love me soon, and if I was already in love with her. I wanted it to happen, and I was going to pray then that we be allowed to love each other, but so many things had failed sadly in my life that I never prayed for a precise, exact thing anymore, especially a woman, because I was usually denied everything. So I prayed, *Dear Jesus, let something good happen in my life. She's here.*

"Your lips are moving," Janice said on my stomach. "What are you saying?"

I was afraid to tell her. We'd only known each other for three days, and even though we'd made love and we got along naturally, and whatever our days *used* to be they now were absorbed by each other. Maybe she'd think I was stupid for praying about her, or that I was some pathetic, maladjusted man, and possibly I was.

"I can't tell you," I said, putting my hand on her cheek.

"Then your lips *were* moving," she said with mild pleasure. "I wasn't sure. Were you talking to yourself? Tell me."

"I can't tell you."

"Kurrrt, you don't look happy. You look so damn sad. You're not supposed to be sad after I fixed you Chinese food and you're at my house holding me in your lap." She grinned up at me and said, "Don't you feel good with an adult woman's head in your lap?"

I smiled. "Yes."

"Then tell me what you were mumbling about. I've decided I want to know you as well as I can, so if you mumble to yourself, I want to know why."

"I wasn't mumbling."

"But your lips were moving. That means you were saying something, like this," she said, touching my bottom lip with her finger and moving my lip real lightly.

I kissed her finger.

"You're a very stubborn man, Kurt. What were you saying?"

So I decided to tell her, in an indirect way, and hope she'd like it.

"I was talking to the son of God," I said.

Her eyes widened a little. "Jesus?" she said.

"Ah. You know his name."

"What were you mumbling to Jesus?"

"I can't tell you. You'll think I'm stupid."

"I will not. And if I do, I'll lie to you and say it sounds intelligent."

"You're funny."

"You're pretty. I want to kiss your blue eyes. Now tell me what you were saying to Jesus, please."

"Okay. If you think you want to know me, you will."

"Of course I want to know you, dammit," she said, rising up on her arm so her face was even with mine. "I wouldn't tolerate you in my home like this if I didn't want to know you, asshole. I wouldn't let you see me with my clothes off three nights in a row if I wasn't utterly, fully, wildly goddamn sure I want to *know* you. Do you understand?"

"I think I sure as hell better," I said, staring into her brown eyes and sighing.

"Yes. You better," she said quietly. "All right. Now you can tell me what you were saying, please."

"Okay."

She stared at me. "Kurt."

"Okay. I was praying. That's all. I don't go to church, for a lot of reasons, and I'm a heretic and I know I'm on my own and that's fine. It doesn't scare me very much, or at least I lie and say it doesn't. But I still pray. I pray every day for things that matter, like you. So while you were lying down in my lap, it occurred to me, just suddenly, to pray that something would work, that maybe something really good could happen to me, and I wanted it to be you. That's what I was doing. I prayed about you. So there."

I closed my eyes so Janice could look at me weirdly or anxiously and I wouldn't have to see it. Now, now would be it. A small panic was settling into me for being honest, for telling this woman I'd only known for three days that I was *praying* about her.

"Kurt," she said, like she was identifying me, or finding me. "Kurt." She put her arms behind my back and pulled herself around me, and as she briefly got on her knees to get a new and stronger grip on me, her feet apparently hit things on the coffee table because I heard my glass of Coke break on the floor and the ashtray fell off, but we weren't in a cleaning mood, and Janice straddled me and pushed me down to the edge of the couch and was lying on me with her cheek pressing on mine as she held my head in both her hands and she said, "Kurt." For a long time we just stayed that way, without talking or moving, and I quit wondering if I was going to be in love with her because I was light and warm and I felt like I was part of her body and part of her breath. It was too late to wonder anymore. She moved up on me far enough to kiss me, holding her lips on mine, kissing the top lip and then the bottom lip and then resting her face on mine, like there had been an exhausting struggle, a search, and now that it was over, we rested. She said, "You have to stay, now. You have to stay."

"Where would I go? You're here."

She kissed my eye and my cheek and said, "I liked you right away when I first talked with you at Annie's party. I was afraid you'd meet some other woman and like her more than me and you'd be gone. I wanted to take you home with me, like this. Kurt?"

"What?"

"Have you thought about falling in love with me?"

"I think I already did."

"You think?"

"You're right. Thinking doesn't do any good. Love isn't rational. Neither am I."

"I'm not rational, either. I think I'll be in love with you before I blink again."

"Blink," I said.

I felt her smile on my cheek. "I blinked," she said.

"Will you make me stay, now?"

"I won't make you do anything."

"Then I'm forced to stay voluntarily."

"Do you want to make love here, or in the bed?" she said.

"Both."

"That's the same choice I was going to make. Take off my blouse."

"I'm not wearing it," I said, and we both started laughing, which, because we were so close, made us bonk our foreheads together. The pain wasn't that severe, and as I kissed Janice's forehead to repair the injury, I unbuttoned her blouse and unfastened her bra, and I just sighed to see her smiling at me and there were her two breasts, and we weren't embarrassed or hurried.

"I tingle when you look at me," she said.

"I do, too."

Slowly pushing me back down with my head on the cushion at the end of the couch, she kneeled over me with her breasts above my face and her legs at my waist, then put my hand on the snap of her shorts.

"You're not finished," she said.

"Oh, God."

"You don't need to pray this time," she said. "And I'm glad you did."

As I kissed one of her breasts and pulled her shorts down and then her panties, sliding them along the smoothness and warmth of her thighs, she lifted each knee briefly to pull her shorts and panties off completely. Her breathing quickened, and so did mine, and before I could unbutton my pants, she moved up on her knees directly over my chest, lowering herself so I could kiss the insides of her thighs. She made a moaning sound, like a girl, lowering herself a little more, until my lips were in the warm, soft dark of her.

# 9

Nothing was more depressing than to be thirty-six, look at your life, and realize you'd reached a workable level of ruin. As a white, male infant born in America during the national copulation project following World War II, when men and women who had postponed sex until toppling the Nazis and the Japanese then resumed the universal urge to make love until exhaustion or daylight intervened, I was ostensibly born with unlimited and unfair privileges. That is, I was white, and I had a penis. Those qualities alone had been enough to assure happy measures of money and power and dominance for millions of white men, and out into the patriarchal workplace I, also, was supposed to go, exploiting and oppressing and, like a cheerful Walt Disney character, whistling as I oppressed. The occasionally provable but also mythical advantages of being a white guy in America were so commonly known and analyzed by the 1970s and 1980s that, sometimes when I'd been applying for jobs then, I imagined just saying to the interviewer: "I don't need a resumé. I'm white and I have a dick."

But I was born naive, a disorder more disabling than leukemia, which my father pointed out to me in 1972 when, instead of going to college to study engineering or computers or business, I told him I was going to study English. He looked across the table at me in the dining room of the Kansas City Club, where we were having a family dinner to celebrate my graduation from high school, and said, "English? You already know English. We taught that to you when you were a boy."

"I'm going to study literature," I said.

"Literature?" he said with scathing distaste, like a bug was on his tongue. "Good Lord, boy. We didn't win World War II and invent nuclear missiles to make the world safe just so people could read goddamn books."

"He's going to be a writer, Daddy," Kristen said, smiling at me.

"We don't need any more writers," my father said. "We've already got Herman Melville and Mark Twain."

"They're dead," I said.

"Dead writers are fine. They write the best stories," my father said.

My mother said, "I don't think Kurt wants to be a dead writer, dear, do you, Kurt?"

"Not right away," I said.

Kristen smiled.

"Well, you're an endlessly naive son of a bitch if you want to waste your life studying literature," my father said.

"I think how Kurt wastes his life is up to him," Kristen said. "Someday he'll be more famous than Dostoyevski."

My father scowled at Kristen and said, "Who's that? Some Soviet defense minister?"

"No. He's a famous dead writer," I said.

"See what literature leads to? Death," my father said.

It didn't lead to death in my case. It only led to anxiety and despair, like being fired from the newspaper, having absolutely no savings, and being forced, out of ugly practicality, to take a job as the toll-free telephone operator who helped the glorious tenets of American capitalism by selling anal-intercourse videos that I didn't think Patrick Henry died for. While I was talking morosely about this with Janice one night, I said, "As an instrument of capitalism, the penis is overrated."

"It has other uses," she said, patting my leg. "You never really believed your penis was going to get you a job."

I sighed and said, "No. In fact, in all of the cover letters and resumés I've sent off in renewed futility this week, I don't even refer once to my dick. I'm too depressed."

Janice hugged me and rocked me and gently laughed in my ear.

"You're a treasure," she said.

"Spend me," I whispered.

"Oh, I will," she said, pushing her cheek against mine and rocking me some more, and I wanted my heart to merge into hers, but there were ribs in the way.

I held her and said, "Janice? Do you want to become one with me?"

"Yes," she said.

"There's bones in the way."

"That's so you can get a grip," she said.

# 10

My crucial break allowing me to resume my damaging career in journalism and acquire important experience I didn't want came to me over the toll-free number at East of Eden. It was an ordinarily slow morning, the time of day when most Americans hadn't had enough time yet to become prurient and depraved and phone in orders for such movies as *Debbie Eats Every Man in Dallas*. To show my boss, Mr. Holstner, that I had a superior grasp of erotic cinema, I suggested that morning while we were both drinking coffee that we could have some attractive and morally neutral woman at the University of St. Beaujolais star in a film we'd produce called *Debbie Puts Fort Worth in Her Mouth*.

Mr. Holstner smiled grimly. "We don't do production. Just sales," he said.

"I'm an artist, Mr. Holstner," I said. "I didn't spend four years in college studying Twain and Dickens and Joyce and Faulkner and Welty and all those other people without first names just so I could sell third-rate pornography. Why can't we take one of our video cameras and do a Tolstoy video called *War and Lesbians*?"

Without expression, he said, "Our customers don't like academic stuff. Put your headphones back on."

I had a headache that morning, as I did every morning when I walked into the little cubicle surrounded by complimentary dildos and vibrators with the catalog numbers on them, as if all of life and history had been reduced to battery-operated love. The four Tylenols I took hadn't numbed me fast enough, so I began massaging my temples with one of the flesh-tone, bendable, three-speed vibrators. I didn't know if it worked for women, but it distracted me from my headache. Then there was a call. I turned the vibrator down to low speed so the customer wouldn't hear it.

"East of Eden Enterprises, catalog office. May I help you?" I said.

"Kurt?" a woman said.

Not many women called, especially ones who knew my name, and a sudden rush of apprehension washed through me.

"Kurt?" she said again, and I began to recognize the voice.

"Janice?"

"Well, of course. I'm probably the only one on the planet who knows you work there, unless you told your sister," she said, laughing.

"Well, Janice, you've never called me at work before. I don't understand. Do you need a portable, pulsating vagina?"

"Stop it, Kurt. The one I have is better."

"I know."

"Guess what, Kurt?"

"I can't guess what. Tell me."

"Some guy named Andrew Christopher called for you at my apartment. He said he's the city editor for the *News-Dispatch* and he wants to interview you this afternoon. I told him three o'clock was fine and I'd tell you. You'll be there. I promised. Kurt? What's that weird noise?"

"I have a headache. I'm massaging my head with a vibrator. It doesn't work very well, either."

"You need a new job. Go."

"I'm going."

The important thing I noticed about Andrew Christopher during my interview in his office in Hampton was that he had a Texas accent and wore cowboy boots, which he rested inelegantly on top of his desk while trying to intimidate me and make me admit that I was a stupid, subservient bastard for coming into his office and needing a job.

"Why should I hire another subservient college boy like you, another spineless clone who thinks he can memorize all the phrases from the *New York Times* and call himself a reporter?" he said, striking a wooden match on the bottom of one of his boots, then lighting a Pall Mall and trying to blow the smoke across the desk into my face.

"Are you from Texas?" I said.

"What the hell would you know about Texas?" he said with moderate irritation.

"At least as much as you. I was born there."

"Well kiss either one of my buttocks and what the hell does Texas have to do with anything?" he said loudly, as if choosing to lose control with me.

"You're wearing cowboy boots," I said. "Most of the people I've ever seen wearing cowboy boots are either Texans or pimps. I'm assuming you're not a pimp."

He squinted at me then, as if sighting me for future damage and violence that might occur instantly, which didn't matter to me because he'd pissed me off enough that already I was imagining how, if he came over the desk at me, I'd shatter the side of his face with my fist.

"I don't think if I was a pimp I'd conduct my business in the newsroom of a daily paper, do you?" he said accusingly.

"You dress too badly to be a pimp. You must be an editor," I said.

This savage remark caught him off guard, and while

he tried to remain haughty and dangerous-looking with me, he reluctantly grinned at me and changed his attitude slightly. Instead of attacking me for my mere presence, he attacked me for sport.

"Boy, I was raising cattle in Texas before you were more than an errant spurt from your daddy's dick on a windshield at a drive-in, and you don't look like a reporter to me, let alone a Texan," he said, blowing more smoke at me.

Tired of the drama, and unwilling to endure his contempt any longer, even if I wouldn't get hired, I sat up peevishly in my chair and said, "From one Texan to another, Mr. Christopher, fuck you. I came here for an interview, not a personal assault. I understand that you want a reporter in St. Beaujolais. I can do that. I've worked for four newspapers in three states for nine years and I know what the hell I'm doing. I've been a copy boy, an obituary writer, a news clerk, and a night police reporter running around looking at bodies in the street just so we could write three goddamn column inches saying one more human was dead. And don't dare accuse me of wanting to imitate the *New York Times* or the Associated Press, because I despise those bastards, which my last editor should be able to tell you if you care to call him."

"I already did," he said, and leaned back in his chair to stare at me suspiciously.

"What did he say?"

"He said he fired you because you can't write good newspaper prose."

"He's mistaken. He fired me because I write better than that."

"He also said you were arrogant."

"He isn't completely mistaken."

And we were both quiet then, privately agitated and silent. My headache came back and I wished I had a vibrator or something. Christopher picked up a filthy coffee mug and sipped from it, then stared off at the wall with annoyed thoughtfulness. Probably I should have just left, but I was going to wait to be asked.

Then, without looking at me, Christopher said, "There's something wrong with you. Something uncivilized. Not docile. Not invaded yet by the horrifying sameness of the world. Whatever's wrong with you is probably valuable. I want to hire you and pay you badly. Is four hundred dollars a week bad enough?"

I said, "Well, I don't get to pick how badly you pay me. You do."

"I want you at work tomorrow. Are you going to ask why I hired you?"

"It's not something I'm willing to question."

Less than two weeks after being fired for who I was, I was hired for who I was. The world had no interest in making sense. That was one reason we had newspapers, to take the ordinary chaos and complexity of daily life, rob it of nearly all emotion and wonder, then arbitrarily force sense onto the world. Again I was going to be an important ally and enemy of newspapers, which I gleefully expressed that evening during a champagne toast to me and my new job, and I wanted to drink. It was embarrassing and oddly sad in this new victory of mine that I couldn't even drink a toast to myself, and I could only watch the waitress uncork the big green bottle that was for me and which I couldn't touch, like it was an old ruin that wasn't done with me yet.

"I want some," I said quietly to Janice, so no one else could hear.

"I know. You can't," she said, squeezing my hand under the table, as if her fingers would help me not want my champagne, and only she and I knew this.

"I can smell it," I said, closing my eyes and still seeing every glass being filled with champagne, smelling the light fragrance everywhere that was supposed to be happy but which for me was just a dangerous taunt.

"Don't smell it," Janice whispered, squeezing my hand harder.

I was going to cry, but not there, not when everyone was happy and couldn't tolerate my sudden breakdown, and so you're dishonest, aren't you, and you don't cry, and you never let anyone know that a panic is invading you again, that a mere fragrance settling across the table wants to destroy you, and maybe you'll let it, squeezing her fingers until you feel bone, and the tiny thump-thump-thump of her pulse in your hand, saying here I am, here I am, and you can't tell anybody, not even her.

Raising my glass. When's it going to go away? Is it? Raising my glass, the only one there with ginger ale in it, as if this makes me safe, deciding not to cry and now invent something you're supposed to say of yourself in a toast, saying, "Here's to that endangered man, me, whose perilous goal it is to, I forget. What's my goal?"

"Not get fired," Janice said.

"Yes. Whose perilous goal it is to disregard the fundamental teachings of American journalism, write however the hell I want, and not get fired."

And everyone clinked their champagne glasses over the center of the table in my perilous honor.

Janice didn't really like the toast, raising up her glass in a new one, holding my chin in her hand so I'd have to look at her eyes as she said, "And here's to realism, which Kurt will have to learn."

"Realism?" I said.

"Unless you want to make a career of being fired, here's to realism, where you actually learn to work *with* editors and not just treat them as your invited enemies," she said.

It was like being shot in the head by the one you love, and such an astonishingly unexpected and accurate shot.

"My God. You just shot me in the head. And you did

it so well, too," I said, staring at Janice and raising my glass until it touched hers, where we held them together for a while and stared at each other, like there was more of her I didn't know and I needed to find it. Find her.

"Here's to realism," I said, not looking away from her eyes.

# 11

The St. Beaujolais bureau of the *News-Dispatch*, my new professional home, was a mildly upsetting brick structure on West Jefferson Street that looked as if it originally was a windowless storage building and was squashed between a drugstore and a vegetarian restaurant.

"What did they used to store here?" I asked my new bureau chief, Lisa McNatt, on my first day at work.

"Men with their pants off. It used to be a massage parlor," she said.

"Ah. From a massage parlor to a news bureau. The building is deteriorating," I said.

"That's why we can afford it," Lisa said. She seemed bright and funny, and already I liked her.

Just like at every other paper I'd worked for, I was given an unclean desk and an unclean chair. On the desk was an old brown phone that looked as if people had thrown it away before but someone else, maybe vandals, kept bringing it back. And I had a brand new computer terminal without a keyboard.

"It's broken," Lisa said. "Christopher said the keyboard should be back today or tomorrow. He's probably wrong. You can use someone else's terminal."

I was briefly introduced to four of the five other reporters who worked at the bureau, all of whom appeared to be in their mid-twenties and seemed so absorbed in their particular stories that day that the rest of reality was an irrelevant distraction. It was reporter's disease, a vile and communicable mental affliction in which a reporter irrationally believes that nearly any given story he's working on for the morning paper is more urgent and interesting than whatever he's *not* writing about, as if all educated and sensible adults in the community based their lives on reading the morning paper. That was dog shit.

Already my sardonic impulses were loose. "Stay. Sit," I whispered to myself, like a dog known for suddenly gnawing on things. And I remembered Janice staring at me seriously that morning on the sofa, smiling with affection and hope, like I was a thirty-six-year-old boy going into the dangerous world again, and she couldn't always protect me. I loved her.

"Do you want to become one with me?" I asked then.

She laughed and touched my face. "I'll become one with you later. You go to work. And try, Kurt, try very hard, to be the kind of reporter they *want*, until everything fails and you bust loose like I know you will. Okay?"

"Okay."

My first official work of the morning was to fix a cup of coffee, light a cigarette, sit comfortably in my unclean chair and say, "It's a good thing I don't have a keyboard, or else I'd have to work."

Lisa sent me down to the police station to read through the daily crime reports, where I saw Captain Trollope and had to explain to him the recent changes in my fate.

"I heard you got booted from the *Journal*," Captain Trollope said. "I was sorry to hear that."

"Being fired is one of those fringe benefits they don't tell you about," I said. "But it didn't last very long. I was hired yesterday by the *News-Dispatch*, and here I am. I guess I'm hard to exterminate."

"Evidently. Did they give you the police beat?"

"I don't know yet. This is just something to keep me busy right now, I think, while they decide which beat I get or if I'll be the free safety."

"Free safety? I haven't heard of *that* reporting position."

"I made it up. It's when you don't particularly belong anywhere, so they put you everywhere. I guess a free safety is like a floater."

This also puzzled Captain Trollope, who smiled and said, "Floater? That's what we call a drowning victim."

"Really?" I said. "I never heard that name before. *Floater.* You cops are grotesque, you know."

"We know."

"But when I say floater, I mean someone who just floats around freely, doing random assignments that no one else can or wants to do."

"Sounds better than a drowning victim."

"I think so. Being dead would interfere with my work."

"Somewhat. Well, congratulations on your new job. If you need anything this morning, I'll be in my office where I don't want you to bother me."

"Well, I'll just bother whoever walks by."

Then I sat at the desk with the big stack of overnight crime reports, scanning each one to look for suitable crimes and peculiarities to write about for the police blotter. There were several DWIs, a tedious feature in newspapers that I despised, as if people genuinely wanted to read the freshest list of strangers who got drunk and drove somewhere. It seemed possible, though, that I could take a group of DWIs and rank them according to how high they scored on the Breathalyzer test. As a journalistic project, I wrote down the names of five people arrested for driving while intoxicated, and included the blood-alcohol levels they got on the Breathalyzer test. In my notepad, it looked like this:

Today's Scoring for DWIs

| Jenny Li, | .22 |
| Mathew Weicker | .19 |
| A. Bobby Carr | .19 |
| Thomas P. Denton | .13 |
| Katherine Poole | .11 |

At the end of the week, the paper could give an award of mild dishonor to that week's most drunken DWI, although maybe that would be too harsh. I'd ask Christopher and see what he thought. If he said we shouldn't ridicule people by ranking their drunkenness, I'd say we already do it by writing about their arrests in the first place. You might as well convert it into a sport.

Most of the crime reports were slight things of practically no interest but which witlessly conscientious reporters wrote down anyway because they're company dullards, such as the report of a woman whose purse, containing car keys and nine dollars, was stolen. I dismissed that crap and searched for things that were at least acutely weird, like this one, written in the officers' own personal scrawls: "Complainant reported apparent sound of cats fighting in her yard, which disturbed her sleep. After I arrived to investigate, complainant complained that my knocking on her door disturbed her sleep. Cats gone."

And this crime report certainly warranted publication for the well-being of the community: "Received call from

Ms. Lohman about a strange man on front porch of her house. Subsequent investigation revealed it was her husband." In my notes, I wrote: "No arrest. Marriage itself not a punishable offense."

Farther down in the stack was a report that most journalists would dismiss as being an empty and vain incident not worthy of serious attention, but to me it was an enthralling bit of weirdness suitable for the front page of the paper, and I copied it all down: "Complainant, Mrs. Delio, advised officers that her estranged husband apparently entered the home in her absence and removed the light bulbs from every light in the house. Complainant advised she couldn't see. Officers confirmed all light bulbs were missing. No suspect."

An instinct or a personal aberration told me that only a meteor hitting St. Beaujolais would be a more engaging story that day, and if a meteor did hit St. Beaujolais, writing about it would be hampered by our instantaneous deaths. Gleefully I went back to the bureau with my prized crime report, interviewed Mrs. Delio over the phone, and began writing a peculiar drama:

> A St. Beaujolais woman's estranged husband reportedly entered the woman's home sometime Wednesday, unscrewed all 19 light bulbs from every lamp and fixture in the house, then escaped with the light bulbs, leaving no clues but the dark.

"Nothing else was gone, just the light bulbs," said the victim, Marianne Delio. "I called the police and told them all my light bulbs were missing. They said buy some more."

It wasn't big or important news at all, but it was funny and human, the kind of story people wanted to read because it wouldn't hurt, scare, numb, annoy, or bewilder them, like the majority of newspaper stories did. The story made it onto the front page of the morning paper, a nice start for my return to a profession that generally regarded me with abiding distrust.

# 12

Insofar as Harmon Sparr wanted someone to be bludgeoned to death with a violin so he could write about it, he was a common American reporter. Harmon, who was twenty-six and had been a reporter for five years, was habitually upset that not enough corruption, evil, and horror happened in Vermilion County to produce the really good stories that newspapers are all about.

"Goddammit," Harmon said in his low, peevish voice as he sat at his computer working on a story about protecting the Wolfe Lake watershed from pollution. "Goddamn watershed. I hate these stories. This isn't journalism. Why can't a military train loaded with five-hundred-pound incendiary bombs crash into a church bus carrying a choir? *That's* journalism."

Harmon's desk was behind mine. "You could go to Romania and get shot to death. I won't stop you," I said.

"Kiss my ass," Harmon said.

"I have a girlfriend. She'd be mad," I said.

"Will you guys please stop talking on deadline? I'm trying to *work*," Rebecca said across the aisle with self-righteous annoyance.

"Why can't we have a revolution in Vermilion County?" Harmon said. "I wish the redneck farmers would attack St. Beaujolais with shotguns and backhoes, a war of genocide against the godless liberals. I'd be a stringer for the *New York Times*."

"You'd be a disfigured corpse," I said. "Farmers hate reporters, too. They'd bury you in a shallow grave and plant soybeans on you."

"Dammit!" Rebecca said, staring angrily at me and Harmon, so we shut up.

One of the phone lines began buzzing throughout the bureau and no one would answer it. It could have been a mayor, a police chief, a provost at the university, a lawyer, a petty bureaucrat, a basketball coach, Jimmy Hoffa. We didn't care. No one liked to answer the phone on deadline, and our secret policy was to ignore it. If you answered, it might be a subscriber wanting to know why they didn't get a paper today. I always wanted to say "Read yesterday's paper again. The world couldn't have changed that much."

I unfolded a copy of the memo we just got from

Hampton. It was from Al Perrault, the executive editor, announcing a style change:

> It will now be the practice of every reporter and editor at the *News-Dispatch* to name the day of an event or action in all news stories at the very beginning of the sentence in which the event or action is described. Example:
>
> "The police Tuesday arrested nine drug dealers."
>
> Many of you are accustomed to a sentence structure in which you would say "The police arrested nine drug dealers Tuesday," which you will no longer be accustomed to at this paper. Instead of writing a sentence such as "Authorities say they received numerous reports of dairy cattle found dead with their reproductive organs missing or mutilated Friday," you will write "Authorities Friday received numerous reports," and so on. The new style, long ago adopted by the wire services, lends immediacy to our reporting.

Immediately I wrote a note on my computer to Perrault:

> Dear Al Perrault: I today got your memo on the style change. I tomorrow will begin using it in all sto-

ries, although possibly I today should start. Never tomorrow put off until today what you can do.

To make sure he didn't get my note, I deleted it, then looked over at Rebecca and said, "Did today you see our new style change, Rebecca? I today don't intend to follow it."

"Shut up," she advised me.

During dinner that night with Janice and Rebecca and Harmon at Collier's, we all practiced the new style, with me saying to Janice, "What today did you at work do?"

She was confused at first, but figured it out. "I today studied some blood pathology charts," she said. "Please all night don't talk like that. I'll get a headache."

"So you don't like journalese?" Harmon said. "All the really important reporters write like that."

"All the dicks write like that," I said.

"Well, you don't have to pay attention to Perrault's memos," Rebecca said. "He writes four or five memos a week. By Friday, he can't remember what he wrote Monday."

"I tonight am glad," I said.

"Don't. I'm getting a headache," Janice said.

"Me, too. Maybe journalism is a virus," I said, putting my hand on Janice's forehead. "Do you ever study the pathology of newspapers?"

"If I ever do, I'll start with you," she said, then looked at Harmon and Rebecca and said, "So how's the newspaper doing with its newest reporter here?"

"It's too early to assess the damage," Harmon said.

Looking at Janice, I said, "They've already asked for my resignation, but I told them I can't find it."

She spit wine, just like when I first met her, laughing with wine in her mouth and spraying it across the table.

"That reminds me of the mosquito trucks that used to spray DDT in Texas where I grew up," I said. Janice seemed terribly embarrassed, and I held her hand under the table as she and I used napkins to clean up the wine.

"I *wish* you wouldn't say funny things when I have something in my mouth, Kurt. And I'm also not sure I like being compared with a mosquito truck."

"I'm sorry. I'll quit comparing you with health-department vehicles."

"But anyway," Rebecca said, giving us a chance to forget about Janice spitting wine, "even before Kurt was fired from the *Journal,* he was regarded as one of the few local reporters who wrote with any sense of style and emotion."

"Which was why he was fired," Janice said. "Do you think he'll survive at the *News-Dispatch*?"

"We hope so," Rebecca said.

"Hope," I said. "I think I need too much hope for one man."

"It'd be a ludicrous mistake for the paper to fire the

only reporter on the staff who openly despises journalism," Rebecca said.

"And if the dumb bastards do fire you, I hope you fire-bomb the bureau and injure dozens of innocent bystanders in town for a world peace seminar. *That'd* be a story," Harmon said.

This jolted Janice a bit, so I had to explain Harmon, somewhat.

"Harmon's not evil," I told Janice, wondering if that was true. "It's just that like about sixty or seventy percent of the reporters in the nation, he wants something repugnant and horrifying to happen because you can't win a Pulitzer Prize for anything harmless."

"That's sick," Janice said.

"It's insane," Rebecca said.

"Those are two qualities that advance careers," Harmon said, staring kind of severely at Janice, then saying to her, "And by the way, Kurt hasn't said much about you at work, but he did tell us you work at the university in viral epidemiology or something, which I think translates into things like herpes and AIDS. So, what kind of secret projects are you working on that we should write about?"

Janice shook her head. "I don't think much of it's particularly secret, or even interesting, unless you're an epidemiologist."

"But you're wrong," Harmon said. "*Every*thing's interesting, with the right angle. What do you *do*?"

"She's not a subject, Harmon. Don't interview her," I said.

"I just want to know what she does," he said, ignoring me. I thought of hurting him. The boy regarded Janice as a potential story, a piece of work. I focused on him like a death ray, thinking of walking around the table and slapping his head onto the concrete floor. I think I smiled dangerously.

"All we do is a lot of tedious statistical stuff," Janice said.

"Like what?" Harmon said.

"Oh, hell, like, well, it's just, for example," she said, "we get pathology statistics, disease statistics from the Centers for Disease Control, primarily on AIDS, and we take these masses of numbers representing the incidence and frequency of AIDS cases in specific areas within a city or a geographical region and figure out where the disease is growing or diminishing and maybe help people predict where it will grow or slow down. It's just numbers."

"But it represents the new plague," Harmon said in a somber and fascinated tone. "We don't have any more Dark Ages rats with fleas killing off the public, but we have AIDS, the new plague. Someone should interview you. May I?"

Janice laughed with confusion or uncertainty, looking at me for an explanation, then just said to Harmon, "We're having dinner. I'm ready for food, not an interview."

"Then later," Harmon said insistently.

I must have been staring at him with such unnerving hostility that he blinked and looked away.

"I won't interview her," he said defensively.

"I know you won't," I said.

# 13

At first it didn't look real when the Harper's Plaza Shopping Center blew up, possibly because I'd never seen a shopping center explode before, so it didn't seem probable. In the night in Wellington County as I drove by, returning from a county planning-board meeting where I suffered severe depression from taking notes on a controversial mobile-home park that I genuinely didn't give a fuck about, a painfully loud and terrifying explosion vibrated me and my car. In the second it took to glance toward the shopping center, about one hundred yards away, a huge, billowy mass of orange flames erupted from the roof of the supermarket. One or two more smaller explosions followed, and as I slammed on my brakes, slid along the highway, and finally stopped at the edge of a drainage ditch, something shattered the rear, side window of my car, spraying little chunks of glass onto my cheek and into my hair. My cheek stung and felt damp, meaning I was probably bleeding. Looking into my backseat for whatever section of the building evidently landed there, I saw a canned ham. I was too scared to be hungry.

Once I realized that almost certainly no one could have been killed or injured, because it was about ten-thirty at night and no one would have been in any of the stores, I hoped, I ran across some grass and up to the edge of the parking lot, as if staring at the burning grocery store from a slightly closer distance had improved the quality of my uselessness then. Orange and yellow flames waved across nearly the entire top of the store, lighting up the huge parking lot so brightly I could see large and tiny shards of plate glass glittering on the asphalt. Chunks and shattered parts of the building lay here and there in the parking lot. Much of the debris looked like groceries, and I spotted near my feet, when I didn't want it or need it, a dented and fizzling can of Foster's lager spurting beer and its powerful odor toward me. I studied it, watching the little geyser of beer, smelling it, knowing that before it was fully wasted I could open the can and hold it in the dark like a vanished enemy who had, ha-ha, found me again. It would never stop looking for me.

But this wasn't the time, however convenient, to resume destroying my life, and I walked away from the spewing can and—why was I thinking *this*?—began worrying about looters. A small mobile-home park was located only a few hundred yards down the highway. I didn't know what I'd do if looters came.

"The store's closed," I'd say.

I noticed my cheek was still stinging, and when I touched it, I felt a sharp piece of glass, not very big, stuck in my cheek. I rolled it out with my fingertip and looked at the fresh blood that trickled down my fingers. I wished Janice was there so she'd be worried for me and fix my cheek and hold me. I liked it when she held me. It came to me that, when I was a boy, if you got hurt and some girl liked you, she'd give you the affection she normally concealed or withheld. Briefly, I thought it was good that I was bleeding because Janice would like me, although she liked me anyway and I wished I wasn't bleeding.

Some people driving by stopped their cars and ran across the grass and up to me in the parking lot. One of them, a tall, fat man in an Atlanta Braves hat, asked what happened.

"It blew up," I said, annoyed that he had to ask.

He seemed breathlessly horrified, then stared at my cheek and said, "You got a gash in your cheek."

"I know," I said. "And there's a canned ham in my car. I didn't pay for it."

I was feeling light and sick to my stomach. Perhaps

shock. I never could remember what shock was, exactly. Probably I was just dizzy. About seven or eight people stood near me and the fat man, all of us holding our hands over our eyes like visors as the building burned, and then I remembered who I was.

"Fuck," I said irritably. "Now I'll have to write about this. Goddammit."

"What're you talkin' about?" the fat man asked a little worriedly.

"A building blows up, somebody expects a description of it. This pisses me off. I'm tired," I said, walking away and back down the grass toward a pay phone at the convenience store across the highway. Andrew Christopher answered the phone.

"Andrew, this is Kurt. Not that I care personally, but the Harper's Plaza Shopping Center just blew up in Wellington County."

"What? Well get your ass down there quick and get me a story."

"My ass *is* down here. It blew up while I was driving by. How convenient. A canned ham broke out my car window and cut my cheek open. I don't think there were any injuries, except me."

"Reporters don't count as injuries," he said.

"Well, put that in the story: No humans were hurt, but a reporter was cut by a flying ham."

For about an hour and a half I remained as a diligent

witness to the rapid destruction of a shopping center, as several dozen firefighters eventually used enough water to cause flash floods in the parking lot and put out the fire after four businesses were leveled. Then I got to go home. Home wasn't my apartment but Janice's apartment, where I arrived at maybe twelve-fifteen in the morning with some gauze taped to my cheek. She was still awake, watching Johnny Carson, and got scared when she saw the gauze.

"My God, what happened to you?" she said, touching my skin around the bandage and making me sit on the sofa.

I put the canned ham on the coffee table and said, "I love it that I can come here and you wonder about me."

"Kurt. What the hell *hap*pened?"

"Janice, Janice," I said, smiling because she was so close and I loved her dark eyes. "On the way back from the planning-board meeting I didn't want to go to, just as I drove by Harper's Plaza, it blew up. Boom. It was a very big explosion, Janice, and just as I almost wrecked my car in a ditch because I think I was horrified and disoriented, that canned ham smashed through my rear window, and a small piece of glass stuck in my cheek. It's not very deep. And look, I kept the ham. Do you like ham? I do."

"Kurt, you look faint. Just lie down," she said, pushing a pillow behind me and making me lie down. She soaked a dishrag in cold water and rubbed it slowly across my

forehead and eyes, and she gave me some Coke to drink.
It was always conspicuously Coke.

"I want some wine," I said.

"No you don't. You don't really."

"Yes I do. That's why I'm not supposed to have any.
I'm tired of being an alcoholic. I want it to stop. Why won't
it stop?"

"You're doing real well. You have to be brave, like you
are."

"Being brave hurts. I wish it would stop."

She rubbed the cold dishrag over my forehead again
and put the soft palms of her hands on my cheeks, like she
was fixing me.

"I'm helping you be brave," she said.

"Yes."

"What did you do, Kurt? What the hell did you do?"

I explained, in my rambling, incoherent way, the im-
pact of the explosion and the ball of fire and how there was
some Foster's lager needing me to drink it and no one
would know, but I walked away, and how, according to the
rules of journalism, reporters weren't human. She liked
the story, even when it didn't make sense, and smiled at me
and laughed, one of the most soothing sounds I'd ever
heard. I told her that. She kissed my eyes. We went into
the bathroom so she could take the gauze off and wash my
cut and put some new goo on it with some new gauze, so
it would be personal. Even though I had a home, a place

where it was said I lived, it was really here. We knew that, and Janice put me to bed with her, covering me with one of her legs and both of her arms and she fell asleep like that. I loved her. That's what I did then, and wondered if in her sleep she knew I was doing that.

# 14

In the morning as I read my story on the front page I discovered that my sardonic joke over the phone to Christopher was placed prominently in the story by Christopher, so that everyone reading about the startling explosion of the shopping center saw this sentence: "There were no injuries from the explosion and fire, except a reporter who was cut by a flying ham from the grocery store." It was a nice touch, and I was glad Christopher put it in. But then the inevitable officiousness and tedium of serious journalism struck like a disease. After our first story with photos ran, and reporters from the afternoon paper, the *Journal*, scrambled that morning to put together a couple of long and annoying pieces about the possible cause of the explosion, what was at first just a pretty interesting shopping-center explosion was transformed by competing editors into the urgent issue of the community, and the two papers began exchanging stories like gunfire to see who could amass the most maddening and essentially unimportant facts. When it was adjudged that a large gas leak from commercial ovens used to bake breads and pies at the grocery had caused the explosion, Christopher ordered Lisa to order me to reach the company that made the ovens, reach the gas company, reach the fire investigators, contact a national association of firefighters in Washington, interview store employees, contact the corporate office of the store, interview the Wellington County commissioners, ask two or three local lawyers if anyone could successfully be sued over the explosion and fires, call other retail bakers in Vermilion and Wellington counties about their ovens, and find out from the St. Beaujolais and Small town halls if they had any ordinances governing safety inspections of big ovens.

We were going to suffocate the readers with facts. But I, the reporter, was the first victim. The editors at our paper and the *Journal* all acted now as if no events anywhere in the lives of the nearly 40,000 people in the community were as important or interesting to our readers as the history of a goddamn blown-up shopping center. Two other reporters worked with me on a daily series of stories on the continuing investigations and the matters of rebuilding the stores and collecting insurance money. For every two stories turned out by the *Journal,* we retaliated with three or four. In a computer message to our executive editor, I wrote: "Dear Al Perrault: Now that we've written ten stories in three days on the shopping center, and we're working on two more, wouldn't it be appropriate to quit calling our paper the *News-Dispatch* and start calling it *Grocery World?*"

On the day that I was trying to write three stories on the shopping center because I was ordered to, I was so pissed off at the untiring dumbness of journalism that I also began writing a sidebar with this headline: "The history of exploding ovens."

Lisa, who saw me writing it and was getting mad because I was mad, leaned over me at my desk and said in a quiet, peevish tone, "Kurt, I know you're pissed off about the amount of attention we've been paying to this shopping center, but it's just responsible journalism to find out as much as we can."

"No it's not," I said with quiet anger. "Someone capriciously decides we'll write about a story and never let it die. If it were responsible journalism to find out as much as we can, we'd do a story on the formation of the Earth and how, over hundreds of millions of years, natural gas was produced, discovered, and eventually used to bake the breads and pies that our readers can't buy anymore from the store that blew up."

"You're pissing me off, Kurt," she said.

"Good. We share that emotion," I said. "I have to finish my story on what the fire marshall says, then begin my three-part series on cakes and pies in North America; plus try to find out if the drop in water pressure as firefighters tried putting out the fire is attributable to poor rural planning for water lines, then call someone from the Institute of State to see if anyone could be criminally negligent for allowing Earth to exist. I'm busy."

Lisa doubled her fist, as if to slug me. Exhaling slowly, she said, "Maybe you need a break. Maybe you should go to Stanley's and have a long beer."

"I don't drink anymore," I said.

"You don't? That's wonderful. But how do you relax?"

"I take my girlfriend's nine-millimeter Beretta out in the country and shoot at army helicopters. Then we go dancing. Relax? Reporters aren't allowed to relax. The world is too urgent. News is too crucial. Now I have to call a psychiatrist at the university to ask if counseling groups have been formed locally to deal with the trauma of exploding shopping centers. The news never stops."

I was quiet, then, and exhausted, and I leaned my forehead onto the cool glass screen of my computer. I felt bad for Lisa, this nice woman who only hoped to be a good reporter and a good bureau chief and who now sat tiredly on my desk, staring at me with a kind of bewildered sadness, and it was my fault.

"I'm sorry," I said, rubbing my head back and forth

on the computer screen, like it was medicine. "You didn't deserve any of that. I apologize."

"You don't need to," she said in a sort of worried tone. "We've been working this story to death. You're right. Sometimes I don't know why I went to journalism school."

"I didn't. I studied English. That's even worse."

"It is? Why?" she said, smiling a little.

"At least with a degree in journalism, people think it's a sensible discipline and you have a moderately decent chance of being hired and taken seriously. People think English is just art, empty crap. Do you know what my first career was when I got my degree in English?"

"What?"

"I was a salad girl," I said.

"A *salad* girl? How could you be a salad girl?"

"Well, I wasn't actually a girl, of course, but I couldn't get a job anywhere, at first. I gradually realized that employers didn't *care* that I had a degree in English, and maybe held it against me. What? You studied *lit*erature? Capitalism has no use for Chaucer or Twain or any of that poetic dog shit about being alive that you so earnestly wasted your time on in college. Boy, was I an extraneous man. So one day, when nobody else would hire me, I got hired in a cafeteria in Kansas City to prepare tossed salads. It was the position of a salad girl, because usually girls or women did it. For fun, I started calling myself a salad girl."

Lisa smiled at me sort of peacefully then, and was

quiet, as if thinking over my stupid adventures as a salad girl, and I remembered I'd been nasty and unreasonably angry with her, so I felt bad for her again.

"I'm sorry for being so nasty. It's not your fault I was a salad girl. I should've known that, by studying English, I was preparing myself for a career in lettuce and tomatoes."

She closed her eyes and sniggered almost silently, then shook her head.

"Don't apologize. You've been having a real bad week, and the pressure at this paper gets damned inexcusable, so don't apologize for getting pissed off at what you *should* be pissed off about."

"Are you mad at me?" I said.

"I'm not mad, no," she said. "I think, like you, I'm exhausted. Do you feel okay, now?"

"If you're not mad at me, I feel okay."

"I was mad at first, but I got over it. Kurt, you're not the only one who thinks this job sucks sometimes. Sometimes I hate it as much as *you* do."

"No, you don't. I've had more experience at hating it than you have."

"Okay," she said. "You hate it more than I do."

"Thank you," I said.

She got off my desk and stretched her arms, then said, "So. Are you going to call the Institute of State and ask if someone could be found criminally negligent for letting Earth exist?"

"Yes. Someone should be in jail."

# 15

Things slowed down in St. Beaujolais, and after an alarming week in which reporters at both papers found nothing seriously wrong, injurious, decadent, stupid, horrifying, or controversial to write about, the weather changed and we had a tornado.

"This is great!" Harmon said exuberantly when he heard the first report of the tornado over the scanner in a warning from the National Weather Service. Jumping away from his computer and the story he'd sullenly been writing about a request for a permit to build a mosque in St. Beaujolais, Harmon ran up to the scanner, knocking a chair out of his way, to write down more details on the tornado. His eyes looked gleeful, somber, and insane.

97

"A tornado. It's mine," he said jealously.

I walked to the scanner to give Harmon some experienced guidance.

"Stupid fucking bastard," I said. Tornadoes aren't fun. They kill people."

"Kiss my ass," he said, scribbling down the reported location and possible path of the tornado. The National Weather Service man said it was spotted touching down in a forest about two miles west of Small, where it was traveling northeast at approximately thirty miles an hour. All of us were gone in an instant, running to our cars to try and catch a swirling, evil mass of clouds that would indifferently destroy whatever they touched. There were three reporters and a photographer running across the street for cars.

"Shouldn't we go in *one* car?" Rebecca yelled.

I yelled, "No. We might all die together. Dying is private, don't you think?"

She looked like she was going to smile, and we kept running. Harmon raced away first in his black Nissan, eager to look at death and ruin, which made front-page copy in any paper in the world. I felt adrenalin and mild, dumb panic while looking up to study the dark gray edges of the thunderstorm swelled above us, but I told myself to be calm. I knew, from all those years in Kansas and Missouri, where all sane people become minor authorities on thunderstorms, that we were on the safe edge of the storm and that the tornado, traveling away from us, wouldn't be here. I bought a Coke at McDonald's. There was time.

The storm and the tornado already had moved far north of town by the time any of us could have gotten onto the Interstate to chase it. There was some very light rain, almost pleasant, while I could see, a few miles beyond my car and over some of the forests on the hills scattered around town, the nearly solid black darkness along the horizon where the storm was still tearing things up. Behind it, to my left, the sun was coming out. Right where the clouds appeared to have been torn away was a rainbow, like a child's drawing superimposed over a vanishing horror. As I thought how pretty it was, I wondered if anyone was dead.

They weren't. No one was even injured, except some pigs and one big sow whose body was found about twenty-five feet up in an oak tree. Highway patrolmen, sheriff's deputies, and other sudden authorities agreed on estimates that the tornado had destroyed itself a path about three hundred feet wide and slightly longer than four miles, missing the few farm homes and mobile homes in the area. Destroying some power lines that weren't very hard to replace, the tornado's main physical effect had been to knock down hundreds of trees in a fairly straight line, after which we had a rainbow. That was how I wanted to write it in the newspaper:

A tornado knocked down hundreds of trees in a fairly straight line north of St. Beaujolais Thursday, after which there was a rainbow.

There were no deaths or injuries from the storm, although a sow weighing about 300 pounds apparently was in the path of the tornado and was propelled about 25 feet into the limbs of an oak tree, where the pig was found dead.

No autopsy has been scheduled.

Back at the bureau, Lisa said no.

"No," she said, shaking her head and smiling nervously as nearly all of us frantically made phone calls and pieced together the unruly elements of two or three tornado stories for the morning paper. "You can't have a rainbow in the lead of a tornado story."

"Yes, you can," I said. "We had a tornado, and then a rainbow. It's factual. I don't invent reality. It's just *out* there."

"No," she said. "I *know* how important it is to you to write well and be distinctive, and I'm glad we have you, Kurt. But no. A tor-NA-do struck."

"And then a rainbow struck," I said. "There was no damage from the rainbow. I think the readers would like that."

"Kurt. I don't want to argue."

"Then stop."

"Take the rainbow out of your lead."

"I like it. It's pretty."

"If you don't take it out, I will."

"All right, all right, goddammit. I'll mutilate the lead. I'll rob it of all the natural wonder and drama anyone would feel and pretend I'm a dispassionate, emotionless reporter armed with dead facts."

"Thank you, Kurt," she said, walking away to her office.

After Harmon realized there were no deaths or injuries, no neighborhoods destroyed, no gasoline trucks burning like in a war, and no mass panic of any sort to coldly describe and win an award for, he soothed himself by concentrating on the forests that were flattened, and the big dead pig in the tree. I walked to his desk to read his lead. It said:

> Although yesterday's tornado miraculously avoided leveling 14 homes in a subdivision next to its path, the afternoon twister flattened as many as 1,000 trees, flung a huge pig into the limbs of an oak tree and caused scattered power outages from downed power lines.
>
> "I think the Lord was watching over us," said Anna A. Lesters, whose home in the Scarborough subdivision was about 20 yards from the edge of the tornado's path. "A tree limb went through the bedroom window, but no one was hurt."

"Idiot," I said.

Harmon was alarmed. "*Who's* an idiot?" he demanded.

"That woman in your story," I said. "A tornado roars by her house, rips up a forest and heaves a tree limb into her bedroom, and she says the Lord was watching over her. I don't know why you'd want to compliment God for a tornado."

"Go away," Harmon said.

"Maybe I should call a priest and do a story on how many people are spiritually grateful for cataclysms, accidents, and disasters," I said.

Harmon smiled at me. "Did you see the pig in the tree?"

"No. I didn't go to that neighborhood."

"It was gross. I'm going to describe it as well as I can," he said with enthusiasm. "Also, look at this, look at this," he said like a boy with a weird discovery to share, and he flipped a few pages in his notebook until he found something.

"Okay. Where is it? *Here,*" he said. "I need to see if I can get this in my lead."

"What?" I said. "I can't read your notes. You write like an inebriated baby."

"This old farmer off the Interstate said after the tornado he walked out to look at his chickens to see if any of them had blown away, and he said he found a dead rooster stuck into the trunk of a pine tree by its beak. So there's this crumpled rooster with its beak driven into a tree, like a nail."

"Wow," I said. "That should definitely go into the story. Tornado lore. Some people will find it offensive, but screw them. All we're doing is describing the world. It's not our fault if reality keeps existing."

Then for a while I just sat at my desk, drinking coffee and smoking a cigarette and realizing I wanted to go across the street to Stanley's and drink some Bass Ale or wine, flood my body and my blood with the secret warm peace that no one could give and no one could share, either, a kind of trapped warm peace, glass by glass until I was numb and kind of distantly serene, where you don't remember you're bones and flesh and nerves and blood that all will leak irretrievably one day and decay and you don't remember being set loose in this world with no more hope than a dog or a bug, waking up each day with stupid dim faith that, before you perish indistinctly and vanish beyond understanding, or touch, or eyes to see you going away, someone will hold you, just you, and say, *Here I am, here I am. I always wanted to know where you were.*

Which scared me then, imagining death again, the final absence of love, I could drink dark warm sherry until being remotely serene even though it was a trick, a wondrous trick leaving me distant both from what I hadn't escaped and from what I hadn't found, although when you drain enough alcohol into yourself that an aura of warmth

swells peacefully inside your head and you can smile without a truth to have caused it, it doesn't matter what you're
distant from. I could advance so far into the daily aura of
warmth secretly in my head that if I were going to serenely
destroy myself, I was the right one to do it. At which point
there was a distant audience watching me, unable to see
my aura now swollen, the peace that, given a chance, quite
patiently kills your need to see a psychiatrist, and I went.
As if, I supposed, asking myself this question: Do you want
to die alone or do you want someone to watch you? You
don't have to die yet. You can wait.

　　You are not, I realized, having fun.

　　So it was decided, I allowed myself this judgment, that
of everything I'd achieved I'd at least achieved being an
alcoholic. This was the wrong career. And I left the psychiatrist and went home where it got darker and darker in
my house, not surprising when Earth turns and it's night,
where I began the sudden and severe discipline, almost a
religion, of withdrawal. Panic me, O Lord, and horrify me,
although plainly I can do it myself. Give me this night this
night this night, I lay me down to sleep and was awake two
days, taking that long before the panic that wouldn't leave
me was finally replaced by exhaustion, and I slept.

　　Now I didn't drink, which itself was a faith, an intense,
private ritual of *not doing*. I taught this to myself. The psychiatrist asked me if I believed in demons. I told her I
wouldn't vote for one. She said, well, the demon you think

you killed in yourself is just you. It's not a demon at all. It's just you.

So you won't exorcise me from myself?

That's death, she said.

Death is a pretty harsh form of therapy. Let's not do that one.

So the demon I tried to kill in myself was only me. No wonder it hurt so much. Still injured and seduced, always seduced by this toxic, numbing peace that no one could give and no one could share, I lived each day in the ludicrous and almost comical triumph of not doing. Like now, I am not having Bass Ale. Now, I am not warm and serene in the aura that patiently annihilates me. And the demon whom I have not killed is not going to meekly vanish, but hides in me, remembering every old seduction and wondering if we're going there again. All I want to do, when every extraneous action and desire is lifted away like a cloak, is love someone who loves me. Looking in her eyes saying here I am. I wondered where you were.

Now, I am imagining Janice. The demon who is only me won't, therefore, go across the street and drink the house wine to resume my tranquil and evenly paced destruction.

I looked at Harmon, so happy and even elated, it seemed, to write with no understanding at all of a lethal force out of control. The only advantage of a tornado over drinking was it worked quicker. If someone found a man crushed to death under a roof smashed there by a tornado, we in the business would strangely assume the death was more notable than the discovery of a man crushed to death from the inside out by his own toxic sanctuary, himself. Horror wouldn't have been so enthralling to Harmon if it were his sanctuary.

I began wondering if a tornado was an act of God. On my computer terminal I wrote: "Acts of God. Ax of God. Does it really seem spiritual to look at mass destruction and attribute it to God? I think we annoy him."

Then I forgot what I was trying to write for the paper. I got some more coffee and lit another cigarette, sitting with my elbows on my desk and the palms of my hands covering my temples and my eyes, like blinders, and thought about the tornado. Soon, I tried to write a sentence on the computer: "For approximately seven minutes Thursday afternoon, a tornado advanced through the woods north of St. Beaujolais, knocking down hundreds of trees that no one should miss because we have thousands more."

That wouldn't work. I was sorry it wouldn't.

# 16

What I had realized about the honorable mission of newspapers in presenting the fullest and freest information for the benefit of all people was that the goal of the *News-Dispatch* was to help push the *Journal* into financial ruin and obliteration. The noble mission of the *Journal* was to tell us to go fuck ourselves. Accordingly, when the alert readers of both papers noticed how we took turns beating each other in publishing any story first, they praised us for our keen and healthy interest in the public welfare, while really we hoped only that the other paper would die so we could mourn them in an editorial and say privately: "You finally folded, you dumb bastards."

If any reporter from the *Journal* got any story or frag-

ment of a story into print before we did, we were politely
scolded and reviled, told that we weren't fully human and
probably had deformed minds. Whenever we beat the *Journal* on a big story or a pointless, disposable fact, we reveled
in smug and ugly arrogance, speculating that the *Journal*
was already a failed paper that hadn't decayed yet. It was
vicious and irrational. It was journalism.

On a Tuesday night when I was covering the Small
Board of Aldermen's meeting because my editors favored
the ludicrous belief that the readers were interested in local
government, Jenny Harbecker of the *Journal,* who I had
worked with before I was fired, whispered to me that she
was going to Wendy's for a hamburger.

"Aren't you afraid you'll miss something important
about this request for a variance on a variance to widen a
sidewalk that had been narrowed?" I whispered.

"I'll let you print it first," she whispered.

"That's mean."

While Jenny was buying her hamburger, the aldermen
voted to change the agenda so that discussion of hiring a
new police chief was raised from the bottom of the agenda
to the next item. It meant not only that I would get the story
in time for the morning paper, but that Jenny wouldn't
even get to take notes on it. This pissed me off at the aldermen, because now Jenny, who was kind of a friend of
mine, would get berated and maligned by that son of a
bitch Justin for missing a story that she couldn't have

known she'd miss. And I'd get a story I didn't deserve, by pure accident. Without skill or virtue, we'd beat the *Journal*, Jenny would be reviled and threatened, and I realized I still wanted to shatter Justin's skull, an evil thought that was still enjoyable. Jenny was going to be hurt and I couldn't stop it, unless I refused to take notes and deliberately missed the story, which I wouldn't do.

The only emotion I had then was anger, and as the aldermen discussed the apparent finalist to be the town's new police chief, Town Manager Gaede announced that the candidate, from Fort Lupton, Colorado, was the only openly gay police chief in Colorado. It was an important detail, one that was followed by silence throughout the room as the aldermen looked at each other and tried not to be silent.

"You mean homosexual," Alderman Delores Newman said, which she shouldn't have because it only drew more attention to the uneasiness that everyone was trying to pretend they didn't feel.

"The preferred word is gay," Gaede said.

And now, Jenny was just getting in worse and worse trouble for not being there, while I accidentally got a front-page story and realized instantly that a lot of people in the area would probably start talking about that queer with a badge in Small. It was a big story, and I felt sick. Even as I took notes, I felt sorry for Jenny, but none of it could be stopped. I went out into the hall with my portable com-

puter and hurriedly wrote a story on deadline about the
only openly gay police chief in Colorado apparently on his
way to Small, and Jenny walked in. She'd probably been
gone only fifteen minutes. She smiled at me and asked if
the aldermen had stopped talking about the sidewalk yet.

"Worse than that, dear. I'll tell you later," I said, and
finished my story. I was sending it over the phone when
Jenny walked back out of the meeting room and looked
scared.

"They just finished talking about the police chief," she
said. "What happened?"

Then I did something reckless and shameful, something that would revulse most serious reporters. I explained everything to Jenny and told her to follow me to
the bureau so I could give her a computer printout of my
story and photocopies of all the notes I took.

She cried. She put her hand over her face and cried
in the hall.

"They'll fire me," she said. "*I* can't go to work *now. I*
can't go *there*. This *ruins* me. It's inexcusable. I won't have
a job." She was still crying and slapped her forehead with
the palm of her hand, then slapped herself again.

I gently grabbed her hand and squeezed it a little, as
if that would help.

"You won't get fired," I said. "You'll have my story and
all of my notes, Jenny. I'll beat you *only* because they
changed the agenda and I got the story in time, which

wasn't predictable and nobody knew it would happen. So you can't get in trouble for that. You can't. So if you just use my story and my notes, you haven't really missed *any-thing*. It'll work, Jenny. And then all you have to do is ask the aldermen a few questions after the meeting and make some calls in the morning and you'll still have your story. Okay? Don't be hurt. It's hurting me too. You're scaring me. Don't do that. You'll be fine."

She stopped crying and looked at me with pink eyes. Her fear was gone, mostly, and she smiled at me with confusion.

"*You're* not supposed to give me your notes," she said. "You're the bastard enemy *paper,* Kurt."

I was so glad she smiled. "Whenever I'm a bastard, I do it on my own. I never do it for the paper. So I'm not the bastard enemy paper. I'm Kurt, okay? Now, hurry up and follow me to the bureau, and don't you *dare* tell any of those fuckers at the *Journal* that I did this or Justin might find out about it and he *will* fire you. Then I'll have to kill the son of a bitch and dismember him and put his vile parts in the regional landfill, which would violate land-use laws and I'd be fined."

# 17

The unspoken image around Small and St. Beaujolais the next day was that a little southern town, Small, might soon have a police chief who had intercourse in the butt. Although the headline on my story said "Small considers gay police chief," it had been suggested in the bureau and on the streets that the headline should have been "Small takes it in the butt." We used the *Associated Press Stylebook*, though, and I pointed out that "takes it in the butt" wasn't the AP style, even though I hated the AP style so much that I wouldn't even shop at the A&P.

Despite the reputation for liberalism and broad-mindedness that St. Beaujolais and Small had, ours was still a fundamentally heterosexual community in a heterosexual world, and people privately winced, I thought, to think of a queer police chief. Almost no one would *say* queer, using instead the genteel expression "gay." But I knew people couldn't help but think that public life was being infiltrated by a man who had intercourse in the butt with other men.

"All this hidden uneàsiness is just weird and stupid," I said, while some of us talked in the bureau.

"Really? Come on, Kurt," Rebecca said. "I've never even *heard* of a gay police chief before, and nobody else has, either. So it's not weird to wonder about it."

"Yeah, but look what we're doing," I said. "A professional lawman was interviewed to come to Small and be a police chief, and instead of talking about whether he'd be a good police chief, we talk about who he fucks. He's not being hired to copulate."

"He's a buttfucker," Harmon said. "I wonder if that's on his resumé."

"I'll ask him when I interview him," I said. "You know, it's a *cer*tainty that when *other* professionals are interviewed here for jobs, they don't say, 'And by the way. Who do you screw? Do you do it with people of the opposite sex, and do you do it in the butt, or what?' It just isn't done. Maybe to be fair, to be responsible reporters, we should call up every public official in town and say we're doing an intercourse poll to find out if how they copulate makes them suitable for public service."

"That'd be fun. Let's start calling," Harmon said.

.　　.　　.

When I tried calling Chief Donner in his office in Fort Lupton, I was glad at first when the dispatcher told me he was in a training meeting and couldn't talk for a while, because I felt stupid about having to interview a man about who he had sex with. While I killed time and waited for Donner to get back in his office so I could interview him, I picked up the phone one time and loudly acted as if I'd just reached Mayor Barbara Sartor in St. Beaujolais and said: "Mayor Sartor, this is Kurt Clausen, with the *News-Dispatch*. We've decided at our paper that since so much public attention is being given to the sexuality of the man who might be Small's new police chief, it's appropriate to find out for the welfare of the public about the sexual habits and proclivities of everyone in public service in St. Beaujolais and Small, so I need to ask you a few questions. Have you ever had intercourse in the butt, and if so, was it pleasant?"

Everyone in the bureau smiled as I hung up the phone.

"You didn't, really," Rebecca said with uncertainty.

"I wouldn't hang up on the mayor like that," I said. "She wasn't home, so I just left that on her answering machine."

Finally, I knew it would happen, I reached Chief Donner on the phone. Before I could ask any tactful or blunt questions, Donner anticipated all of them.

"I know," he said in a pleasant and sort of deep voice. "It's the obligation of the press to examine my law enforcement credentials, my ostensible success as a police chief here in Fort Lupton, and other pertinent questions about anal intercourse."

It was so sudden and astonishing that I laughed.

"Well, I'm glad you have a sense of humor," he said. "I know everything you're going to ask. I've been interviewed dozens of times by all the local papers here."

"No, you don't know what I'm going to ask," I said, realizing it was safe to be whimsical or ironic with the man, instead of distant and cautious.

"Sure I do. You're going to act like it's part of the finest tradition of American newspapers and democracy in general to ask me all about being a police chief in relation to how and why I have intercourse."

He was right, but in my deliberately absurd style, I said, "I wasn't going to ask you any of that. I was going to ask if you ski."

"If I ski?" he said, starting to laugh.

"Yes. You're up there by the Rocky Mountains, so I knew our readers would want to know if gay police chiefs ski. Do you?"

He did laugh, then. I was glad.

"You're not like most reporters," he said.

"Not really."

"Well, yes. I do ski," he said.

"Downhill?"

"It's too hard to ski uphill," he said.

"I wouldn't know. I don't ski," I said. "But I used to live in Denver, when I was a boy."

"Really?" he said. "You lived in Denver but you never skied? That's criminal."

"Criminal? You mean it's illegal in Fort Lupton to not ski? I'm writing that down, chief. None of the other papers have this stuff."

Eventually Chief Donner and I digressed to the subject of his being a gay police chief, which didn't seem upsetting to him at all.

"Fundamentally, it's best not to care a great deal if some people are going to want to call me a queer and say public officials shouldn't have sex in the butt," he said.

As I was writing that sentence down in my notebook, I said, "Chief, that's a great line, but you know we can't print that."

"Why?" he said. "Do you mean that all of those people in the public who have images of a police chief having sex in the butt would be horrified to see their own imaginations in print?"

"That's it," I said. "I think they object to their own knowledge."

# 18

Things soon broke loose, and I was one of the fragments. On the same day my interview with Chief Donner was printed, the *Journal* ran a story saying there had been dissension and even a brief walkout among police officers in Fort Lupton when Donner became chief there in 1984 because some officers didn't want to work for a queer. The *Journal* printed a huge headline saying, at the top of the front page, "Dissension revealed in gay police chief's department." It was a sensationalist story hinting at fractious troubles to come if Donner was hired by Small, and it essentially repeated an old story of problems long ago worked out between Donner and the officers in Fort Lupton. But because I didn't have the same story, Lisa angrily told me what I'd done was shoddy, incomplete reporting that embarrassed the newspaper because we were beaten by the *Journal.*

"Fuck the *Journal,*" I said in her office. "They took an old incident that was big news five *years* ago in Colorado only, one that involved maybe six police officers and which was resolved in a few weeks and hasn't recurred. So what's my embarrassment to the paper? That I didn't exaggerate the fuck out of an old incident and pretend it was urgent news?"

"The embarrassment is that you didn't have it at all," Lisa said with quiet anger.

"I had damn near everything *else* in the interview."

"Everything else doesn't matter. What you *didn't* have matters."

"Jesus Christ, Lisa. That's like telling me that *most* of what I did was good, but because I didn't have some old news from Colorado that doesn't matter anymore, I screwed up the whole story."

"It *does* matter," she said, and threw a phone book at the wall. "It's the main reason we're even writing *stories* about this guy! He's a gay public official, and if he comes to Small to head the police department, he might run into some of the same problems he had in Colorado."

I didn't want to argue anymore. My head hurt and Lisa decided I was wrong no matter what.

"That's in my story," I said quietly. "Three or four

paragraphs of information and quotes from him saying he knows he could have those problems, but he doesn't think it could be serious and he'll be able to deal with it if it happens."

Lisa exhaled loudly and looked away from me. "But you didn't get the story about his troubles in Colorado," she said.

"I missed it. You're right. I only got how he'd deal with it here. Kill me."

Lisa scowled at me. "Put it in your next story," she said.

"Oh boy. One more story about the gay police chief and what he does with his butt."

"Don't push me, Kurt. Don't."

Also that day, Al Perrault had written a wildly ignorant editorial with all the grandeur of enlightened homophobia. It was the true embarrassment of the paper, one that made me ashamed to be a reporter there. Like looking at a dead animal on the side of the road just to see what it was, I looked at the first two paragraphs of the editorial again:

> It shouldn't surprise anyone these days, with AIDS spreading like a cancer, that we have a homosexual police chief in Colorado. But do we need one in Small?
>
> It's hard to say if discipline and morale will be damaged among the well-trained male police officers

in Small if the Board of Aldermen elects to hire a homosexual to lead them. We've all heard stories about valiant homosexuals who fought in World War II, Korea, and Vietnam. It seems appropriate, then, to keep our minds open now as a body of elected officials examines a prominent homosexual who has sex with men.

Janice called me at work and said she'd just read the editorial.

"Kurt, it's too embarrassing to be in print," she said.

"I know."

"I'm writing a letter to the editor."

"Don't use my name," I said.

"I won't. The first thing I'll say in the letter is it's fantastically stupid to say AIDS is spreading like a cancer. AIDS is spreading like AIDS."

"I know. Perrault's stupid."

"You sound depressed, Kurt. Are you okay?"

"No. I'm a reporter."

"What's wrong?"

"I went to work."

She laughed a little bit and said, "Kurt, please don't feel bad. It's Friday. Do you want to go to the mountains?"

"I don't know."

"Yes, you do. You want to go to the mountains with

me. We'll stay in a lodge and go hiking and no one will bother us all weekend. Say yes."

"Yes."

"I love you, Kurt."

"I'm glad. I love you, too. I want you to hold me, now."

"I can't hold you over the phone," she said.

"Goddamn phone."

"You're silly," she said. "I'm going to pack some stuff after work. I'll be ready when you get home."

She'd never said that before. A pleasant, kind of scary shudder or tingling went through me. "Home?" I said.

"Yes. Home," she said. "I said that, didn't I?"

"Does this mean we have a home?" I said. "I want it to."

"Kurt. This is odd. I said home, like you're supposed to be there."

"I know. I realize that. I like it a lot. You'll be ready when I get home."

"That's right. When you get home," she said.

"I'll try and leave work early."

"Good."

The day wasn't through annoying and injuring me yet, though. Bobby Havelock, the mayor of Small, called to excoriate me.

"I want you to know that I'm very angry and I think it's both unprofessional and irresponsible of you to have written one more story that dwells on the sexuality of Chief

Donner rather than his splendid record as a police chief, and I'd recommend that you resign," the mayor said.

Oh fuck. "I didn't dwell on his sexuality. I wrote about it," I said.

"When Don Hoyle was hired to be the police chief up in Cokesboro, I didn't see any strenuous efforts at investigative reporting or any sensational articles on *his* background or where *he* came from," the mayor said irritably.

"He's not gay," I said.

"Is *that* it then?" he said with more anger. "These are supposed to be more enlightened times, and I find it singularly repugnant that you'd single out Chief Donner solely because he doesn't choose to have vaginal intercourse."

"I don't care what kind of intercourse he has. He gets to pick."

"Don't be haughty with *me,* goddammit!"

"I'm not haughty. If I wanted to be haughty, you'd *really* be pissed off. And don't accuse me of singling out Donner for anything more than being a gay public official in an overwhelmingly heterosexual world. That's news, and I don't invent news, as much as I'd prefer to."

"Well, I'm damn sick of this so-called news, where a decent, intelligent, exceedingly competent man is held up as a public curiosity just because he's homosexual."

"I'm sick of it, too. *I* didn't want to write the goddamn stories. It's not *my* fault that having gay police chiefs is a social novelty. So quit being pissed off at me. Be pissed off at humanity."

"I'm calling your publisher," the mayor said in a sullen tone. "I think your entire bureau should resign."

"I'll tell them, unless you want to call everyone individually."

I heard him bang the phone down. Very slowly and quietly, I hung up the phone, sighed, and stared at the ceiling. Everyone in the bureau who had heard my part of the conversation—four reporters and Lisa—walked toward me, the way water comes back after a splash.

"Who was that?" Lisa said.

"Some mayor," I said.

"Havelock," Harmon said solemnly. "What'd he say?"

I wondered how to summarize everything I was already trying to forget. "Ohhhh," I said, "something about newspapers, enlightened times, anal intercourse. We were just chatting."

At home that night Janice said an odd irony about me writing about Donner was that while the public was being asked to wonder, through my story, if a homosexual could be a competent, acceptable kind of human, the public had no idea that the story about the homosexual was written by an alcoholic.

"It's like the public itself always takes on the general pose of goodness or wholesomeness," she said, "and when

an issue like homosexuality comes along, represented here
by a gay police chief, the public is asked to pretend to stand
back objectively and examine the whole subject of homosexuality through the presumably objective, untainted,
wholesome institution of the daily paper, as if you, the reporter, represent all of the unquestionable goodness of the
public or something. But if the public knew you were an
alcoholic, you'd be in the same damnable position as the
gay police chief, or worse. Its almost gotten fashionable
among some people to accept gays and lesbians, or at least
say you do. But if you started telling people you were an
alcoholic, people would secretly think of you with pity or
revulsion, as if you weren't Kurt anymore but you were just
a drunk."

Even though what Janice was saying was correct and
she only said it because she cared about me, it hurt me to
listen to her. I was afraid to look at her, as if even some part
of *her* couldn't help but find me detestable.

"Kurt. I'm not *saying* you're a drunk."

I couldn't look at her, reminded—and she didn't want
to hurt me—that all my life now I wouldn't really be
thought of as a man you could talk with but just this hu-
manlike figure with symptoms of life.

"Don't." She walked from the kitchen and kind of
kneeled next to me on the couch, putting my head against
her chest and holding me.

"You're okay," she said, squeezing me to her.

"Usually when people tell you you're okay, it means something's wrong with you," I said.

She rocked me a little and held me and said, "Kurt. Shut up."

I did.

# 19

As we drove west into the stinging brilliant light of the afternoon sun, Janice wore black sunglasses and a pink, straw sunbonnet, which made me decide she looked like a nursery-rhyme girl planning to attend a robbery.

"Does that mean I look exotic?" she said.

"It means you're pretty," I said, watching her drive. It was pleasant and soothing just to look at her, to see her leg and her arm work together when she shifted, to see her do anything, and to take me with her.

"I like it when you're in control," I said, resting my hand on her shoulder.

"All I'm *doing* is driving," she said.

"I like it when you're driving, and I get to be with you."

She reached over and stroked my cheek with her fingers and we kept going into the sun. Fast. She started to tell me which mountains we could go to, but I asked her not to. I asked her not to tell me which mountain or mountains or *part* of the mountains we were going to, so it would simply be up to her and we'd just drive up in there and be at a place and that was it. The mountains.

"Okay," she said. "Kind of like we're going into a life that hasn't started yet."

"Yes. But it will," I said.

"I know," she said, and she put her fingers between mine and rested our hands on her leg. Soon, she started singing "Old MacDonald Had a Farm," like a girl on a long trip.

"You're such a girl," I said. "I love it."

She smiled and kept singing the various verses, and when she asked me to sing with her, the first verse I sang was "and on his farm he had some pigs / and committed sod-O-mee."

"Kurt," she said. "That's not nice."

"I know," I said. "In some states, Old MacDonald could be arrested for that."

"You've been a reporter too long," she said. "You're cynical and jaded."

I smiled and put my head on her shoulder, saying, "Then fix me, woman."

"Oh, you big baby," she said. "We'll be in the mountains soon. We'll find a nice place to stay and we can hold each other."

"Drive faster," I said, and she did.

# 20

The mountain we were on we called This Mountain, after the respected tradition of arbitrarily and abruptly naming a mountain anything you wanted because no one could stop you. Janice knew the real name of the mountain but she promised not to tell me. I was tired of facts, tired of precise knowledge and one more thing to memorize and clutter my cluttered head.

"It's just you and me, Janice. No facts."

"Very well," she said, like someone in a British movie. "We'll just proceed with innocence and ignorance, the qualities we have at birth."

"I still have them," I said.

"You're not innocent," she said.

129

"Well, I still have one of them," I said.

She laughed, and said, "So do I."

We were walking up the little dirt trail toward the top of the mountain, holding hands, and Janice said, "This Mountain is a good name for this mountain."

"Yeah. See how well it works?" I said. "A hundred years ago or something, people probably stood on this mountain saying, 'What should we call this mountain?' And I'd have said, '*That's* it. Call it This Mountain.'"

"Sometimes," Janice said, "you're alarmingly brilliant."

"I'll be quiet."

"Don't. I don't like it when you're quiet."

We both were in astonishingly good moods, like exuberance, one of those words you think you know precisely but actually you just say it because it hints at what you are. But Janice kissed me on the lips real hard and said she was just exuberant and that I looked the same, so we decided we were exuberant. It was about ten in the morning, Saturday, and we made love at the hotel and took a nap, then here we were on the mountain, just walking up this trail because there was a trail and it went up. Something we didn't say, didn't speak, the way you did with most observations, was that we were in love with each other and we knew it. It was as if this had to hit us spontaneously at the same time, and you could just tell, you could sense it. It was as plainly there as if a big breeze came up, and we didn't have to say to each other 'The breeze is here.' I could look into her eyes for the longest time, and she'd stare back, like we were entering each other. We did that once on the trail, just stopped walking and were about a foot apart and stared into each other's eyes, as if there were something we had to say that language was no good for, so even if you talked about it, it would just sound stupid. Janice sighed, and then I sighed.

"This reminds me of the only line from the Bible I've memorized," I said. " 'The heart sighs when it's too full for words.' "

She looked surprised or astonished or something, then smiled at me real delicately and hugged me.

"I'm glad you were born," she said.

It made me start to cry, not like I was hurt, but that I wanted this woman so badly and there she was, and she wanted *me*. I didn't know why. I kissed her hair and tried not to cry, which wasn't working completely.

"Don't cry. I have you," she said. "And you have me. See how nicely that works?"

"Yes. It keeps working."

"Don't cry, Kurty," she said, kissing my ear.

"Kurty? When did you start calling me Kurty?"

"Just now, Kurty. I think it fits you."

"Even if it doesn't, I can tell you're going to keep calling me that."

"You're right, Kurty."

And up the trail we started again, side-by-side under a brilliant hot sun, with no more precise a goal than reaching the top of This Mountain so we could look across at the surrounding mountains and feel wondrously remote from everything but each other.

On the long walk up, I started singing, for some reason, the lyrics to "Michael, Row the Boat Ashore."

"He rowed the boat ashore on a mountain?" Janice said. "Sounds like Michael got lost."

"Yeah. He was a rowin' son of a bitch, that Michael."

After about an hour of laborious but kind of pleasant walking, we were at the fairly flat, slanted top of the mountain where we expected to be able to look off for ten or fifteen miles in any direction and see all the other huge mountains. But all there was immediately around us were more trees.

"Well, god*dammit,*" I said with exaggerated annoyance. "We climb up six thousand feet to the top of a mountain to get a view of the *trees* growing up here? Janice, there's something seriously wrong with this state. The only place they don't have trees is in the ocean."

"I think you're right," Janice said as we stared around at the forest. She took her camera from her backpack and said, "Stand there in front of those trees. I want to get a picture of you at the top of the mountain where you can't even tell it's a mountain."

"Okay."

"And try to act like you're real high up, so people will know," she said.

"I'm real high up," I said, and she took my picture.

We did some brief exploring and stuff and finally found a big rocky area with almost no trees at all where we could look off into the vast, hazy distance where dark mountains rose and drooped into each other gently.

"And look! Real cliffs!" I said happily, pointing at the massive rocks where it looked like you could easily fall and die. "Mountains aren't real unless they have huge cliffs where you can fall and die. Boy, I bet you could fall a thousand feet from here."

"Let's eat some sandwiches first," Janice said, grinning at me.

"That's right," I said. "You don't want to die on an empty stomach."

"Let's sit over here on the rock, since all there is is rock," Janice said.

"You're a realist. I like that."

She had fixed us some peanut butter and grape jelly sandwiches, which we ate with Fritos as we stared off at the sloping, jumbled mountains that looked as soft as velvet, except for an open spot here or there where you could see some kind of little building or part of a road. Sometimes we'd see a hawk or an eagle drifting way off in the faint blue sky, just floating and not really appearing to have anything in mind, except floating.

As Janice stared off at some of the distant bigness, I tried to calculate which part of it she was looking at so I could look at it, too. I wanted to see what she was seeing. I told her that. She smiled and patted my cheek, like I'd done something pleasant.

"You're such a child," she said, kind of matter-of-factly. "Do you know that? Here we are on the top of a mountain, staring off miles away at mountains and shadows and clouds, and when you realize I'm looking and wondering at some very particular thing out of all that, you want to see it, too, to see it *with* me."

"I do not," I said, lying. Then I suddenly looked down at some ants on the cliff and said, "See that ant carrying away the leg of a dead grasshopper? I was looking at that."

She smiled. "Kurt, you're such a boy," she said. "A wistful boy."

"Wistful?" I said, wondering if she knew that or if she was guessing. "I shouldn't be wistful now. I'm with you."

"That's what I keep telling you. When are you gonna know that, Kurty?" she said, and scooted around on the rock behind me, putting her legs around my waist and pulling me to her so my head was right under her chin.

"What do you know about me that I haven't told you?" I said.

"That you're sad," she said. "It's one of the things I

first knew about you. When I met you at Annie's party, and we started talking for such a long time, and you made me laugh. You were so funny, and you hardly even smiled, like it was something you knew how to do, that you'd studied very well, but it didn't always make *you* smile. And you'd always get this sort of remote, wounded look, as if a lot of bad things had happened to you and they hadn't really left you. At first, you just worried me, like who *is* this weird, sad guy who keeps being so suddenly funny. And then, I don't know why, you quit worrying me and I just thought you were charming or something. So I waited to see if that would wear off, and it didn't. You were so damn funny and endearing. When you got quiet, I'd look at you, and you were sad again. I wanted to kiss you."

"You did," I said, nestling my head against her chest. "I was glad."

She put her hands on my stomach, one hand above the other. "What happened to you? What makes you sad? Did bad women hurt you?"

"Not really. Most of the women who hurt me were good women, but that's part of it, yes. I'm used to being in love and being abandoned that way. I don't really blame anybody, or say they're wrong. But it happened to me three or four times in the last ten years, and I don't think I ever really recovered completely. I'm bad that way. Maybe I'm just weak. I don't know. I think I hurt too well. Like if you're born with an acute ability to feel emotions real hard, and real long, I'm one of those guys. I have a genetic or spiritual disorder. I hurt too well. And each time I always lost somebody again, I'd try to remember that stupid, stupid saying, 'Time heals all wounds,' like it was supposed to work for me if I just thought of that saying. But it didn't work. Lying bastards. It didn't work. Although, actually, maybe it never had a chance to work, because I lost consecutive women. Maybe you're supposed to only lose *one* woman, and feel *that* agony, and then you get over it and find someone you don't lose. I did it completely wrong. I lost three or four in a row. All that ever really mattered to me was to love someone who loved me, and every time I found someone, they left. It was like the world, or some god, was dispassionately looking at me and saying, 'I know what we'll do. This'll be neat. See that guy down there who hurts too well? Three or four times in a row, we'll let him fall in love. And just when it begins to work and the woman is part of his own spirit and he loves her so much that, at night when she's sleeping, he likes to breathe her own breath, like it's a gift, right then, we'll make the woman realize he's the wrong man and abandon him, abruptly taking away everything that matters and replacing it with nothing. *Then* he'll hurt, and get good at it.'

"And I did. I don't want to be good at it anymore," I said, and held Janice's hands on my stomach. She began swaying very slowly, from left to right. I realized she was rocking me.

"That's a very mean god," she said. "Do you think it's still happening?"

"I don't want it to be."

"Do you still pray? Pray about me?" she said, still rocking.

"Yes," I said.

"What do you pray?" she said, sliding her hands up to my chest and very gently squeezing me.

"I pray that I'll get to love you, and that you won't go away."

I could feel her sigh. My head rose up on her chest and she sighed. "That's a good prayer," she said. "I won't go away, Kurt. I'm glad the other women did. Not because it made you so sad, but because here you are, and I get you. In return, you get me. Is that enough?"

"Enough?" I said. "I don't think of you as being enough. I think of you as being *it*."

"It?" she wondered. "Kurt, that's so impersonal when you're trying to say you love me. *It* is when you can't identify something, like 'Eww, what *is* it?'"

"Okay, you're not *it*, then," I said. "I didn't mean to compare you to something you'd find on the side of the road. All I mean is I love you, and quit trying to trick me into saying that."

"I love you, too, and quit telling me which tricks I can

use if I feel like it. I'm your best friend and your lover. That means I get to be as maddening to you as I want, because you'll always want me."

"I don't know if it's *fair*," I said skeptically as she rocked me. "But if we get to madden each other, at least it's equal."

"Already you're maddening me," she said.

"I'm fast."

# 21

Now that we'd sort of formalized our love for each other and were happy about being alive, we sat on the edge of the cliff and talked about dying. Janice sipped some red Italian table wine from her thermos, and I drank Coke from mine and smoked a Camel Light. We sat with our thighs touching and our legs dangling over the cliff that went almost completely straight down for maybe three hundred feet or more to where there was a small outcrop or something, and we couldn't see how much farther down the cliff went. Being on a cliff always reminded people of death, so we talked about it.

"Death is stupid," Janice said.

"I know, like calling it names will embarrass it," I said.

"Death is an asshole," she said, smiling at me.

I decided it was my turn to say slanderous things about death. "Death is such a dick," I said.

"Have we libeled death?" Janice said.

"I'm not sure. I have an AP stylebook and libel manual at work, but I've never read the part about libel. That's because I think if you're really good at libel, you don't have to read a book about it."

Janice laughed, and wiped some sweat from her eyelids. We stared down at the tops of pine trees so far below us that they almost looked like moss, or shrubs.

"Do you know what I hate about death?" Janice said, taking a sip of wine and reaching for my cigarette.

"That it exists?" I said.

"That, too," she said. "But let's say death is going to exist and you can't stop it. Nothing, so far, will prevent it. What I hate then is that death doesn't care how or when it destroys. A baby might die thirty seconds after birth from a malformed heart. It might die at seventeen from being drunk and falling off a hotel balcony during a prom. Or you could live to be eighty and choke to death on soup. It's not like death is some noble, mystical force that we should learn to deal with. Death is just this capricious, random killer," she said, frowning and looking at me for agreement.

"Now you've libeled death," I said. "I think libel means when you deliberately attempt to injure someone's reputation and livelihood."

"Death doesn't have a livelihood," Janice said.

"You're right. Death doesn't get paid. So that can't be libel. It's probably just slander. That's not as bad as libel. We're fine."

"I'm glad we're fine," she said, patting my leg and sniggering. "But do you believe in resurrection, now that I think of it?"

"Oh, Janice. Don't get me started on religion. I'll just get pissed off and slander everybody in the Bible, and then on Judgment Day, I'll have to have *two* lawyers with me. I'll get Jewish lawyers. Supposedly they're smartest. And when it's time to go before God and be accountable for everything I did in life, my lawyers will say, 'Your honor, our client doesn't remember all that. Also, we request a delay in judgment, allowing our client time to sneak to the back of all of humanity and hope you forget he's here.'"

She stared at me with astonishment, and laughed. She said, "*Kurty*. Some people just com*mit* sins. I think you in*vent* them, really. I'm gonna have to watch out for you, my God."

"Okay. I'll be quiet."

"No you won't. You never are. That's one thing I like about you. There's almost nothing quiet or resigned *about* you."

"You either," I said. "That's why you can tolerate me."

"But I don't understand," she said, staring in my eyes.

"You're so," and she was quiet, wondering which word I was.

"I don't know which word I am, either. Don't think of it. You'll hurt our feelings."

But she kept thinking of it, finally saying, "You're so skeptical, and mocking about religion, as if it has all these obvious, stupid flaws that you won't tolerate. And despite that, and the fact that I know you don't go to church, you still pray. You pray about me, and I'm glad. But I don't understand. How can you be so skeptical but still you pray?"

I was quiet, wondering about that. "Yeah. It's very weird," I said.

"But I know," she said. "I used to go to church, since I was a girl and until I was maybe eighteen. I went to college and met atheists."

I said, "See? College is bad for you. I think we should outlaw education. It would protect our ignorance from corruption."

"I'm not an atheist," she said.

"I remember the first time I met an atheist. It was at some party in Johnson County, Kansas, and I was drinking a beer and talking about some kind of philosophic crap you talk about when you're in college. And this guy said he was an atheist. I said, 'Really? That's not much of a religion.'"

"Will you *stop* it?" she said, laughing and trying not to. "Quit interrupting me. I'm trying to ex*plain* something to you, dammit."

"Okay."

Janice looked puzzled. "Now I forget which thought I last forgot," she said.

"It was about atheists in college," I said.

"That's right. But that's not what I'm getting at. I gradually stopped going to church, too. But not because I'd lost faith in anything. It was just that church was so *strange*. They created an entire atmosphere of, for me, complete, inscrutable weirdness. It was as if each instant of life, whether you were eating breakfast or playing outside or looking at your dog or anything, was either movement toward sin, or away from it. I just thought it was crazy, that every instant of life had to be religious, and if you weren't memorizing the Bible or spending every scant second directing your thoughts toward Jesus, you were some repugnant, lost person. Actually, I began to wonder, just a little, if Christianity itself wasn't pathological, and not me. So I backed out of that. But I still believed in God. It was like, God was there, somewhere; I always assumed he was in outer space, beyond our telescopes, but somehow, religion got in the *way* of God. It became this sort of spiritual bureaucracy, I guess is the best way to put it and sound irreverent, this church, dogma, pathological bureaucracy saying all that mattered came from the Bible, and anything not focused on that was evil. I couldn't take it. So I excused myself from organized religion. And what I realized I'd done was keep believing in God, because I wanted to, but I wanted him to be a better God than the one at church, you know? I didn't want some god who was supposed to be omniscient but who didn't even know Adam and Eve were going to eat that apple. Which means he either *isn't* omniscient—and that makes Christians look stupid for saying he is—or even worse than that, he isn't love, and I get so mad when people say he is. How can you call it love when you let Adam and Eve eat an apple that supposedly starts a chain reaction of biological sin throughout the entire history of humanity? That's not love. That's an epidemic. And I don't like it, dammit, and you're not going to get me to go into a building where they have an organ and a choir and people dressed up beautifully to sing songs about someone who started an epidemic."

She looked suddenly bewildered, like she hadn't known she was going to say all that, and she shook her head and smiled at me, saying, "Now do you think I'm terrible? Please don't think I'm terrible."

"I think you're great," I said. "I think you're even more heretical and skeptical than *I* am. Although I won't call that a public honor. But now we'll never get in fights about which church we won't go to. We both won't go to the same one."

What she told me as she set up the tent, which I watched because she knew how to do it and I didn't, is she wanted to do something in life that really mattered, before she died, and maybe nothing mattered.

"That is, maybe you don't go to heaven or you aren't reincarnated and you just, like bacteria or a plant, fall away and see no more," she said.

"Like bugs," I said.

"What scares me is that most people, and I've done this too, just go through rituals and routines every day, like you have a job because you need money, and you have a husband or a wife because you need companionship and sex, but all you're really doing is acting out these rituals and routines because you were taught to do that."

"I wasn't taught how to set up a tent," I said. "That's why I'm standing here."

"And sometimes I just get really godawful scared, and I don't know why I'm telling you this now, it just came to me, like I can trust you with this," she said.

"If you can't, shoot me. We brought the gun."

"But sometimes I'll feel this sudden panic in me, like an anxiety attack, but it's not really an anxiety attack, or maybe it is."

"I've had anxiety attacks. It doesn't matter if you don't know what to call them. They hit you anyway."

"And I'll just feel deeply, deeply scared, like why the fuck am I alive? Why am I *being* here right now, hearing sounds and seeing things and being this woman named Janice? As if I'm supposed to *know*, like there really *is* an explanation and I'm supposed to find it, because do you know what'll happen? One day I'll just die, like we all do, and if there's nothing *out* there, if you just vanish and all your emotions that ever mattered are permanently ended, I better do something that matters now, if this is all we have."

She stopped tying a rope on the tent to look at me kind of sadly, and I walked over to her and we held each other. I said, "Maybe we'll vanish slower this way. And let's don't talk about death for a while, okay? I know we're both going to die, but if we keep talking about it, we should set up our tent at a funeral home. Which reminds me: why do they always set up tents at funerals? It always makes me think you're supposed to have a buffet and maybe play croquet on the lawn. Cemeteries are too nice just for graves. You should be able to go there for a burial and to play baseball."

# 22

"Do you think we should shoot something to death for dinner?" I said, holding Janice's Beretta straight out with my left hand and squinting down the sight into the trees just beyond the tent Janice had set up on some weeds and flowers not far from the cliffs.

"We *have* food," Janice said as she tinkered with our fire and looked at all the various hunks of semirotten wood we'd gathered to keep a big fire burning all night and scare away bears and tourists.

"I know. But this country was settled by people who went out and shot something to death for dinner. Being in the wilderness reminds me of that."

"Well, you don't look like a pioneer. Pioneers didn't wear Cleveland Indians baseball caps and carry Berettas."

"I'd be one of the *elite* pioneers. We dress better, and have neater guns."

"Kurt, don't shoot anything."

"I'm an American. We're *supposed* to shoot things. It's part of the true pioneer spirit. We didn't come over here for religious freedom. That's bullshit. We came over here to steal land and shoot things. Sounds like Germans, doesn't it? But it wasn't. It was the English and the Spanish, mostly. Best goddamn thieves of the seventeenth century."

"Put the gun away, Kurt. If anything attacks us to-night, you can shoot it. I think we better fix these steaks now, before any more bacteria has a chance to grow on them and give us food poisoning."

"It *is* like the pioneers," I said cheerfully. "Our dinner might make us sick."

"That's right. We could have fevers and severe intes-tinal cramps together. What a special night, just the two of us, groaning and crying."

"If another woman ever asks to have cramps with me, I'll tell her no. I only do that with you."

"I swear to God," she said, shaking her head and laughing. "You're the strangest man I ever knew. You don't even re*mind* me of anybody. I'm glad I met you in time to steal you from the women who abandoned you. Kurt, put the gun down and come over here and kiss me."

"Yes, ma'am," I said.

. . .

Even in the summer it got cool in the mountains at night, and we wore jackets and sat on big rocks I found and put next to the fire. The dark was so thick and heavy around us it almost seemed like a force, or a presence, instead of just the absence of light. The closest town, wherever it was, was obviously hidden on the other side of some mountain and was so small that no lights radiated up into the night sky, and it was like civilization didn't even exist, or was concealed in the pure dark. Our fire was a big one and a hot one, with a dozen or more limbs, all of them fat, crisscrossed over each other and producing brilliant, soothing flames. It also created a wobbly kind of sphere of light that encircled us and seemed like our protected domain. Janice drank some red wine, and I had some brown Coke, and we looked out of our sphere of light up at the unimaginable glittering of stars that looked permanently strewn across the dark, like God got a handful of stars and threw them, and they stayed there always, scattered for our wonderment. Which made for good poetry, until scientists told us the stars were made of hydrogen. No one wrote poems about hydrogen. Janice told me since I thought of it, I should. The century was changing things. When lovers looked up at the burning hydrogen at night, it wasn't as romantic. And carnal love had changed, too, Janice said. It was almost completely synonymous with viral infections, now. So at night, if you were in a bad mood, or an ironic one, you didn't look up at the twinkling stars with your lover. You looked up at seething globs of hydrogen with your vector. I said, "Vector? What's vector?" She said a vector was an organism that transmits disease, like AIDS. Oh. That. You mean in the spring, a young man's fancy turns to vectors? It's too sad. Don't say that. I won't anymore. Not much poetry was going to come out of hydrogen and vectors.

Into the dark we stared, beyond the cliff and beyond the next mountain, where everything competed to be darker and more absent.

"It's void and without form," Janice said.

"It's void where prohibited," I said.

"If you look straight up at the stars, where there's supposed to be some hope and wonder, it just makes you feel small and sort of pointless."

"Sounds like we should be writing a pamphlet to help people despair."

"If there are hundreds of millions of stars in the universe, which scientists say there are," she said.

"They're just guessing. Those fuckers can't count."

"And you couldn't even get to a single star without being killed by it. Why do people say stars are proof of God, as if He made things you either can't get to because they're too far away, or they'd kill you if you got near them? Is that divine?" she asked.

"No. It's just inscrutable. You can't scrute it."

Then she drank some of my Coke, the way she did

sometimes to be intimate with me and to take communion with me, because it was kind of religious that I'd decided never to have alcohol again or slip even once into the easy euphoria of dry sherry or Bass Ale. The psychiatrist said if I did, I'd want it even more and more, and this time, maybe, if I wanted it to, it would devotedly kill me.

And so like two priests, Janice and I sipped my Coke, a kind of personal religion with just us in it. And as we spoke abruptly and spontaneously, sharing the things that secretly passed through us then, she just said, "It was an important accident that I met you. I could've gone to any of several universities, but I wound up in St. Beaujolais. I could have left North Carolina for various jobs long ago, but I stayed here. And I also could have gone with some of my friends to this country-western bar in Raleigh the night I decided instead to go to Annie's party where, by accident, I met you."

"It makes me sound like a useful mistake," I said.

"That's not what I meant," she said. "You *are* useful, though."

In the dark, thick, jumble of trees beyond us and everywhere came the hooting of owls, chatting to each other or whatever they did, talking about some rodent they were thinking about eating. Certain pieces of wood in the fire popped and had little explosions, making bigger the wide trail of glowing embers wiggling up into the dark, where we watched them vanish, like the night eating fire.

We always put one more limb on the fire, and another one, to keep the sphere of light big around us, and the warmth.

A snapping sound came from the woods, like a solid limb breaking, and we both jerked around to see if something was coming at us, but there was just darkness. We stared at each other, trying to see how afraid we were, or if it was funny, and I picked up the gun.

"It might be a bear," I said, and we were both silent, listening hard. But there was a breeze making noise, and some owls way off, so we couldn't hear the padding, giant footsteps of something out there that we hoped was going away.

"Kurt?"

"What."

"Remember when I told you earlier not to shoot anything?"

"Yes."

"It's different, now. If it seems reasonable, shoot something."

"Okay."

There had been only that one snapping, and no more noises like it, and I wished the breeze would shut up so we could hear. Janice put her arm around mine and drank some more wine, staring into the big darkness as she drank.

"Camping is supposed to be fun," she said. "It's not fun thinking something might kill you."

"We won't die. It was probably just a skunk," I said, then thought of everything it could be. "It was probably just a skunk, or a weasel, or a raccoon, or a possum, or a wild boar with tusks the size of hunting knives."

"Stop it," she said.

"Or a bear, or a bobcat, or maybe Big Foot."

"Or maybe it's Elvis," she said.

"Elvis? I never did like his music very much. I'll shoot the fucker. He'll be dead *this* time."

"You wouldn't really shoot Elvis, would you?"

"If he comes out of the woods singing 'Viva Las Vegas,' I will."

We squinted into the woods some more, and Janice put two more limbs on the fire, making everything a little brighter, except for the darkness around us. She looked at me holding the gun and said, "I just thought of something. Do you know how to use that gun?"

"Not really."

"That's what I thought. You better give it to me. I went to a shooting range in Raleigh. I know how to aim it and actually hit something."

"But, Janice. I want to shoot Elvis."

"You haven't been trained to shoot Elvis. I have. Give me the gun, Kurt."

So I gave her the gun and she put it down near her foot. It didn't seem like whatever was going to kill us had any real interest in us anyway, and it looked as if the night was going to resume being just the night, leaving us alone. Janice got out her miniature Sony TV, and it was impossible not to giggle at each other for having a TV with us.

"This is fun, going to this much trouble to get away from civilization and then watching TV in the wilderness," Janice said.

"I know. It's silly beyond redemption. I like it."

She fiddled with the antenna for a while until some show came in.

"'Gunsmoke'! This is great!" Janice said, and we sat together on the ground watching James Arness shoot people with his polite reluctance.

"We have a gun, too," she said girlishly, holding up her Beretta and comparing it with Matt Dillon's revolver. "This one has a lot more velocity," she said. "Plus it's prettier."

"I have a shooter, too," I said, putting my hand between my legs.

Janice grinned at me with her lips tightly held together. She put the palm of her hand over her mouth so she wouldn't laugh.

"You'd have to wear the holster in the front," I said.

Her head was trembling a little bit, and it looked like she was biting her hand.

"But I'd hate to walk into a saloon where they made you leave your shooter at the door."

She laughed, toppling backward in the dirt. Her voice was so pretty when she laughed, and I realized I was elated to be able to cause that in her. Sometimes I could be elated just by looking at her. She was a lot.

When she sat back up, she leaned her head against mine and hugged me, sniggering a little more and putting her hand between my legs.

"I like your shooter better than mine," she said. "I'm glad you brought it."

# 23

At my desk in the bureau Monday morning, I was sore and tired and filled with a kind of silent exuberance. Vivid pictures of Janice appeared and disappeared in my memory, automatically, like my heart was showing me what mattered, and I sat there quietly at my desk, watching. No one else was in the bureau, and the phone buzzed.

"Fuck you," I said, waiting for the phone to quit buzzing. The noise seemed to drive away the automatic pictures of Janice, and I was angry at journalism for doing that. My normal impulse was to never answer the phone anyway. Lisa established a rule to answer every call within six rings. No one honored the rule. We established a separate rule to answer within six minutes. The phone wouldn't quit buzzing, so I answered it.

"*News-Dispatch*. Kurt Clausen speaking."

"Yeah? Well, where's my morning paper?" said an old woman, with deep spite.

I hated it when strangers assumed I was worthy of being abused by them.

"I can't find it, either," I said. "It's not here."

"Well, that carrier of yours is worthless. How am I expected to read my paper if I can't find it?"

"I'm not sure, ma'am. I think the Massachusetts Institute of Technology is working on that project. One day, you'll be able to read something that's not there. These are exciting times."

"If my paper isn't in my driveway in ten minutes, I'll be calling you back."

"Yes, ma'am."

I resumed sitting quietly at my desk, wondering why I was loose in the world, when I'd see Janice again, and how long I could endure being a hard news reporter before the maddening sterility of it poisoned me and drove me into a state of depressed panic, like Victorian housewives suffering hysteria. That was why Justin fired me. I had no will to write orthodox news anymore, or to cover any of the annoying human events that rose above the usual tedium of daily life, distinguishing themselves as news not because they were worth knowing about but because an editor said so. Papers lied when they said their mission had anything to do with describing human events that mattered the most. Their missions were to master uniformity and sameness. If they inadvertently reported something that more than thirty percent of the readers really cared about, which was unlikely, it was nearly a certainty every time that each competing story began with the same facts, the same emphasis, the same wording and the same phrases. The key wasn't that the readers were being given a story that meant very much to anyone, but that the reporters and editors were getting more successful at reducing all existence to a uniform, deadened sameness, like cells duplicating themselves.

At my desk I typed this note:

Reporter's Workshop, June 23, Washington.
<u>Dare to be the Same.</u>
Panelists from Columbia University, the University of Kansas, The New York Times and The Washington Post will work in small groups to help new and experienced reporters master the skill of sounding like everybody else.

Harold K. Wasserman, 18-year veteran at The Times, delivers keynote speech: "Sameness Makes the Difference."

Call 202-639-1002 to make a phone ring.

I pinned the note on our bulletin board, where I noticed a new memo from Perrault:

When reporting on prominent homosexuals, always refer to them as homosexuals, not gays. "Gay" is the preferred euphemism that we don't prefer. When reporting on prominent heterosexuals, it doesn't matter, so you needn't allude to what kind of sex they like.

Whenever I imagined Perrault, I imagined a man in hiding from his brain. I assumed he rose to the position of executive editor through a profound accident we weren't encouraged to know. Like a senile czar, he retained his title and some access to authority, part of which, I hoped, was secretly taken away from him each time he tried to use it.

Back at my desk, I wondered what I'd write that day, and why. If Lisa was in a bad mood, or if her sense of abstract professionalism overpowered her sense of humanness, she'd probably order each of us to write two stories; not because there were that many stories worth writing on any given day, and certainly not because you could turn out two superior stories in one day. You usually couldn't. But because the *Journal* had the asshole rule of forcing its reporters to turn out two and sometimes three stories a day—regardless of how incomplete and sloppily written such stories almost necessarily were—Lisa sometimes forced the same rule on us, the way a military officer would impose hardships on his troops, as if the goal no longer was to excel at a single story but to show the readers how many items we could cram into the paper without justifying why we did any of it.

It was about eight-thirty, at least half an hour before anyone else would be in, and in my luxurious privacy, I began drawing a chart on my pale purple legal pad:

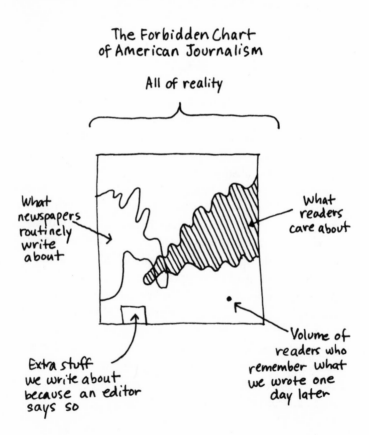

The Forbidden Chart of American Journalism

All of reality

What newspapers routinely write about

What readers care about

Extra stuff we write about because an editor says so

Volume of readers who remember what we wrote one day later

The chart needed refining. I didn't have time to do it because I needed to start planning my next story that not very many readers would be interested in. Regardless of what story I selected, if I began working on it assiduously and did any of the interviewing or writing before the ten o'clock staff meeting, and Lisa didn't like my idea, the story would be held or killed. So if I began working now, there was at least a fifty-fifty chance of accidentally wasting my time by working. If I deliberately wasted my time and did nothing, I'd still get paid the same amount of money as if I accidentally wasted my time.

Faced with that, I went to McDonald's to buy a biscuit.

Having part of a dead pig in my mouth reminded me of a story I could work on: The vegans!

# 24

On my McDonald's napkin, I wrote "Dead pig in mouth. Vegans." This was to result in one of my eternal skirmishes with editors. Newspaper editors mainly believed that the only subjects worth unquestionable attention were government, politics, education, crime, and disaster, as if the remainder of life were peripheral. This was, I knew instinctively, dog shit. The vegans were fascinating, and despised dead pigs in your mouth. I didn't care that Lisa or any other editor would sneer at this idea and regard me again as a precocious but regrettably whimsical reporter. This was *life*, not news. Editors often acted as if news were the most refined form of reality, when actually it was just a goddamn side effect.

Why, then, are you a newspaper reporter?

I'm not. That's just my title. They have to call me something.

In the ten o'clock staff meeting, after everyone else announced their appropriate stories for the day, covering government meetings, criminal proceedings, school-board ramblings, a house fire and university affairs, it was my turn to propose my coverage for the day.

"Dead pig in mouth. Vegans," I read from my napkin.

Lisa blinked at me. "Does that mean something?" she wondered.

"It means the vegans are attacking. They've killed pigs," Harmon said.

"Vegans don't kill pigs. They only kill plants," I said.

"And, how is this a story?" Lisa said. "Aren't the aldermen discussing a road-widening project with the DOT?"

"Yes, but roads aren't as interesting as dead pig in your mouth and vegans," I said.

"We need to find out which roads will be widened, how much it will cost, how many trees might be cut down in the right of way and all that stuff, plus ask someone if the project might threaten a rise in property taxes," Lisa said, which was like saying to me "Shut up, Kurt."

"We already know some of that stuff and the project won't start for at least six months," I said, which was like saying to Lisa "I know more than the news, and no, I won't shut up."

Then I explained vegans to her. "Vegans are people who don't eat meat or any animal products, for moral and environmental reasons. Some of the local vegans, who object to dead pig in your mouth, are having a meatless Fourth of July picnic to draw attention to dead pig in your mouth and why it shouldn't be dead or in your mouth. They'll have fake hot dogs and fake hamburgers made out of soybeans. It's grotesque. I'm sure the readers will want to be outraged by this."

"Kurt," she said with exaggerated patience. "The road-widening story is clearly a more substantial piece of news."

This was the mental disorder called journalism. But I couldn't say that to Lisa. I had to try to honor her authority, even though I didn't honor it, and use tact and guile to avoid writing about some goddamn roads.

"Road," I said. "Dead pig. Dead pig on the road. I sense a union of ideas."

She smiled at me with annoyance. "Can you do *both* stories?" she said.

"If I'm coerced."

"You are."

"You're an evil woman. Do your sins ever upset you?"

"Not at work," she said.

An old realization visited me again as I went to my desk. We frequently didn't select stories because they had some obvious or immediate effect on the public. We se-

lected them because we felt like it. This was important, and
I composed it on my typewriter:

*Another maxim of journalism:*
*News is anything we say it is.*

That went up on the bulletin board. Then I went to
my desk to try calling various vegans named in a press release about the meatless Fourth of July picnic, which the
vegans were calling Independence-from-Flesh-Day. On
the third call, I reached a woman named Kathi. Her last
name wasn't listed in the press release. When I told her
who I was and that the press release didn't list her last
name, life became strange again.

"A last name is a yoke to the past, a form of cultural
and spiritual bondage robbing you of genuine identity,"
she said.

"Oh," I said, since I thought it was the safest remark.

"My last name is gone," she said.

"That's an interesting last name," I said.

"No. I'm afraid you misunderstand me."

"Not really. You gave *up* your last name, and now you
only have a first name."

"That's correct."

For a while, I invaded her privacy and her life, asking
her any questions I cared to think up for any reason, without justifying any of them, because that's what reporters
did.

"Why do vegans think it's wrong to put dead animals in your mouth?" I said.

"Because animals are sentient," she said.

"Not dead ones."

"No, but animals shouldn't be killed for food. They have an awareness of being alive. We believe it's immoral, actually, to kill animals for food."

"Then if a catfish eats a crawdad, the catfish is immoral?" I said, taking notes.

"No. Catfish don't *have* morals," she said.

"I know. They're probably promiscuous. But that's not really the point. The point is, if it's immoral to eat animals because they're sentient, then couldn't you say that half the animal kingdom is immoral because they eat each other?"

"No, you can't say that," Kathi said without her last name. "Animals don't have morals, so it's not wrong for them to eat other animals."

"Oh. Oh," I said. "So if a Bengal tiger killed and ate me, that's okay, but it would be immoral for me to eat a Bengal tiger, because he's sentient."

"I think you're twisting my logic," she said.

"No. I think it was kind of curved when I received it. Let's quit using the word 'moral' and just use the words 'good' and 'bad.'"

"All right," she said kind of warily.

"Okay," I said, because that's how all classic intellectual

arguments begin. "It's bad to eat animals because they're sentient."

"Yes," she said.

"Well then, when all the animals in the world eat other animals by necessity, it's bad."

"You're trying to *trick* me into saying that nature is wrong, aren't you?" she said.

"Well, I wouldn't say a trick is necessary. If vegans say it's bad to eat animals, then they *are* saying nature is wrong."

"Mr. Clausen, I did *not* say that," she said peevishly.

"No, but your reasoning says it."

"I refuse to be interviewed," she said, hanging up the phone.

Still, I had a legitimate story to write, one that would piss off all the vegans and vegetarians in Vermilion County. Sometimes reporting was fun. To add balance and depth to the story, I called an ethics professor at the university to chat about vegans.

"Is it immoral to eat hot dogs?" I said.

"Hot dogs aren't sentient," she said. "Is that the answer you're looking for?"

"Yes, ma'am," I said. "Then I can quote you as saying 'Hot dogs aren't aware of themselves?'"

"They don't even know they exist," she said.

"That's a wonderful quote. Thank you."

In the morning, as I ate breakfast with Janice, we both

looked with delighted astonishment at my front-page story in the paper. She read the first few sentences aloud:

"The hot dogs people will eat by the thousands this Fourth of July once were aware of themselves.

" 'Yes, you could say that putting part of a slain pig in your mouth, in the form of a hot dog, is the same as eating a creature that once was sentient,' said Kathi, one of the local vegans planning an Independence-from-Flesh Day picnic in Vermilion County.

"Kathi (who legally abandoned her last name) is among a growing number of vegans and animal rights activists who believe it's wrong or immoral to kill animals for food.

" 'Animals are my friends, and I don't eat my friends,' Kathi said, attributing the quote to George Bernard Shaw."

"That sounds sexual," Janice said.

"I know. I don't eat my friends. I don't even lick them," I said.

"You lick *me*," Janice said.

I was embarrassed, then leaned over and licked her nose.

"That's not usually how you do it," she said, grinning.

"I was raised not to have sex during breakfast," I said, staring back at her.

Her eyes narrowed a little bit as she grinned. Putting

her spoon down, she stood up in her peach nightshirt, pushed the table away and stood over me in the chair, straddling my legs and pulling up her nightshirt high enough to lower it back over my head, like a tent. By standing on her tiptoes, she arranged it so her warm stomach was right in front of my face.

"This is the best tent I was ever in," I said.

"I'm the mysterious circus lady. See what I have for you?" she said. She sighed when I kissed her stomach, and didn't say anything when she rolled her white panties down and stretched up higher on her toes. She was always a new gift.

# 25

One day, for no defensible reason, which was often how life progressed, the Ku Klux Klan decided to have a parade in St. Beaujolais to promote white pride and piss off all the liberals. I called Mayor Havelock in Small.

"There you are being overshadowed by St. Beaujolais again," I said. "I bet you were pretty disappointed when, one more time, St. Beaujolais gets the parade."

"It's an honor to be snubbed by the Klan," he said.

"Sure. You don't even have any hotels or convention centers for them," I said.

"I don't have time to be bothered by you all day."

"It doesn't take that long."

Harmon was nearly elated that sullen Klansmen with

guns in their pickups were coming to town. "If everything
works right," he said, tapping his forefinger thoughtfully
on his lip, "angry blacks and lunatic college students will
call the Klansmen motherfuckers and failed descendants
of the apes. Rocks and Molotov cocktails will be thrown.
Innocent people will die needlessly in a bloody horror
that'll be shown on the 'ABC Evening News.' I hope it
doesn't rain."

St. Beaujolais Mayor Barbara Sartor issued a formal
statement saying although the Klan was not welcome in St.
Beaujolais, their presence couldn't be forbidden without
violating their civil rights.

"On the day of the parade," her statement said, "I urge
all residents of St. Beaujolais to stay away from downtown,
granting the Klansmen a parade and no spectators. To be
greeted by a ghost town would be the welcome they deserve."

Harmon and I were assigned to cover the parade. Harmon said if I got killed, he'd write about me. I said if he
got killed, I'd steal his car. Janice reacted to the parade with
mild anxiety and depression, telling me to always stay as
far away from the crowd and the Klansmen as possible, and
to please not die on her. "You come home to me, dammit,"
she said, staring real hard into my eyes; not that I was in
any known or likely danger, but that when she even imagined me dying, it scared her. I told her I'd always come
home to her.

On the afternoon of the parade I wore basketball shoes, in case I had to run, and jeans, a black, short-sleeve shirt, sunglasses, and my Cleveland Indians cap. Captain Trollope, who was accustomed to seeing me in a dress shirt and necktie, squinted at me with amused uncertainty.

"You look like a drug dealer," he said.

"It's just a weekend job," I said.

He and I stared off down West Jefferson Street at about forty or fifty of his uniformed officers standing along both sides of the street for several blocks. They all wore helmets. Trollope said another thirty-five or forty officers from Small and the county were available, on standby, plus some highway patrolmen. Barricades had been put up at both ends of the parade route to keep cars off the street. Pedestrians were allowed to walk on the sidewalks, but only a dozen or more people were out.

"Is everyone staying home?" I said.

"I hope so," Trollope said.

It was an extremely hot, sunny day, and Trollope had a bottle of Dr Pepper. I had a Coke.

"I've never seen a Ku Klux Klan parade before," I said. "Do they have batons?"

Trollope glanced at me and looked away. "Well, in the old days they didn't," he said. "They just wore sheets and carried crosses and things. But they're always trying to change their image. Maybe now they have batons."

I drank some Coke and smoked some of my cigarette, then said, "Will they be driving go-carts?"

Trollope sniggered and wiped some sweat from below his eyes. "I think they'll just be walking," he said. "They don't have a permit for go-carts."

"Oh. This is a pretty primitive parade," I said.

"Yeah. Pretty basic."

"Do you think any of them will bring musical instruments, like accordions?" I said.

Trollope put his fingers over his mouth and laughed.

"They wouldn't seem so sinister if they played accordions," I said.

"Then I wish they would," Trollope said.

It was about quarter of two. The Klan was supposed to assemble and begin the parade at two. It looked as if maybe another five or ten pedestrians were on the sidewalks down the street, but there was really hardly anyone gathered, except cops. I saw Harmon. He was sitting on top of one of the one-story buildings down the street, shaded by a tree big enough to do it.

"Well lookit there," I said, pointing at Harmon. "There's Harmon, on top of a building."

Trollope stared at him. "What's he doin' up there?"

"I think he's hiding. He wants to see a violent parade, but evidently doesn't want to be in it. Could you get one of your snipers to shoot a limb off over his head?"

"I could ask," Trollope said, holding up his walkie-talkie.

"Or just throw some tear gas at him," I said. "Harmon loves tear gas. It's his favorite fragrance."

"Tear gas is expensive," Trollope said. "It would be more economical to just shoot him."

"Well, if that's all you can afford, okay."

It was sort of fun, waiting for the Klan. Kind of like a party that shouldn't have been happening. The television camera crew that had been standing in the shade of the Pizza Hut awning walked over to Trollope and me with the refined or unavoidable look of self-importance that most TV news guys had, as if reality didn't matter unless they got it on tape. The reporter was Cindy Kudzil, who everyone called Cindy Kudzu. As Kudzu approached Trollope with her microphone, I said to him secretively, "Don't talk to her."

"Why?" he said quietly.

"Just to piss her off."

The camera guy aimed the camera at Trollope as Kudzu asked Trollope where the Klan was. He delicately dabbed some sweat from his forehead with a paper napkin from his shirt pocket, then said, "Well, they're scheduled to show up pretty soon. But we don't insist that they do."

"Do you anticipate much trouble or violence?" Kudzu said.

Trollope shook his head. "We have some background on these boys, from the State Bureau of Investigation and so on," he said. "I estimate they'll be less dangerous than a crowd of well-bred, law-abiding college students overturning cars after a big basketball victory. Generally, the Klan behaves better than college students."

I was writing that down and smiling. To show my grasp of the severity of everything, I said to Trollope, "What if the Klansmen start playing basketball?"

"I hope they don't become that violent," he said.

Kudzu seemed irritated by my presence. Looking at my black shirt, sunglasses, and Cleveland Indians cap, she said, "Are you with a paper?" Actually, she meant, "Get the fuck out of here."

I wondered what lie to tell her.

"I'm an agent with the Bureau of Alcohol, Tobacco, and Fireworks," I said, then looked away, as if preoccupied by the seriousness of everything. Kudzu and the camera guys walked down the street, probably saying bad things about me. Trollope and I immediately resumed standing there pointlessly, waiting for some ignorant dickheads in sheets to hold a parade in a town that despised them.

"Do you think they'll wear sheets?" I said.

"I don't know. Sheets, or those army camouflage clothes. I think the sheets are a little dressier."

"Yeah. They're more formal. At work, we were wondering where the Klan gets their robes. It was suggested that they bought them at the KKK-Mart."

Trollope grinned, and sipped some Dr Pepper. I wondered if the Klan wasn't going to show up at all; if some delays or accidents or loss of interest would harmlessly cancel the parade, which would have been fine. I didn't want to work on Saturday anyway. I could've been working on a story to send to *The Paris Review,* or out at Baker Lake with Janice, or watching a baseball game on TV with her.

"I hate this shit," I said.

"You mean being here?" Trollope said. "I thought you reporters loved this shit."

"*I* don't love this shit. We're standing around wasting our goddamn time, sweating on a summer day, waiting for some mean-spirited, ill-tempered, dangerously ignorant dickheads to exercise their civil rights in an asshole parade meant to express hatred toward anyone who isn't like them. I'm not entertained. Maybe the fuckheads got lost. I wish they would. And no one would look for them. We'd send out blindfolded search parties. They'd come back and say, 'No. We didn't see anything. Guess they're lost.' That'd be a fun story to write: Klansmen lost: Blindfolded searchers unable to find them."

Trollope took the last sip of his Dr Pepper, then said, "Well, I'm sorry. Here they come."

I looked to my left and thought it was Halloween. Eight or nine men wearing billowy white robes and pointed hoods walked slowly down Jefferson Street in our direction.

"That's not enough for a parade," I said. "And look. They don't even have batons. These guys don't know *shit* about parades."

As I quickly began taking notes and Trollope casually spoke into his walkie-talkie of the appearance of the Klansmen, another ten or eleven men, mostly in robes, came into view from up the street, as if all of them had parked their cars or trucks far out of view and came onto the street in two groups that now were assembling near Trollope and me in the middle of the street. I counted nineteen Klansmen. They didn't seem to have guns, but I wondered what was in those robes. One of them carried a crudely constructed wooden cross in front of him, a cross about five feet tall that appeared to have been made by someone to whom carpentry was an alien profession.

"I don't see any accordions," I said. "You'd at least think they'd bring balloons. What a sorry parade."

All of the men looked angry and sullen, as if those emotions armed them against this town and the contempt they expected to find here. An angry crowd, though, could never have shown as much contempt as an absent crowd. And that, mainly, was the kind of crowd waiting for the Klan. Maybe twenty-five people were on the sidewalks behind all the cops on what otherwise was a pathetically empty street. If the Klansmen had wanted to feed their hatred and anger on the ugly emotions of a crowd, they weren't eating today.

"This is neat," I said. "They want somebody to hate them, but no one's here. I bet they feel cheated. This is wonderful. Those dicks."

The Klansmen, who looked to range in age from the early twenties to the fifties, arranged themselves in parallel columns, with the cross guy in the front.

"What do you call the cross guy?" I said.

"I don't know," Trollope said. "You could call him the cross guy."

"That's the same title *I* was thinking of," I said, writing it down in my notepad. Several of the Klansmen held placards made of large rectangles of cardboard fastened to thin wooden handles. People with bad handwriting and lettering had composed various messages on the placards, such as "Give the government back to the REAL PEOPLE: WHITE CAUCASIANS."

"That's not fair to the black Caucasians," I said, still taking notes and squinting at the placards for more slogans, none of which were particularly good and most of which were thoughtfully savage. One of them said, "There is a cure for AIDS: Kill Queers."

You had to start thinking that these people weren't people. Such violent hatred couldn't come from humans. But actually that was one of the emotions that no other animal had; the will to exterminate their own kind. I tried not to look at that placard anymore, but the other slogans were nearly as irrational. One slogan was "Liberty and justice for <u>ALL</u> doesn't include everyone."

I wondered who it left out. Another slogan was "Let our children pray in school! Put God back in the classroom!"

I looked at Trollope and said, "Why does God need to go to school? I thought he was omniscient."

Trollope just shook his head and lit a cigar, staring with a kind of patient annoyance at those potentially dangerous Halloween guys whose presence forced most of the entire police department to work on a Saturday to protect the Klansmen's rights to dress badly and publicly share their absence of humanity. Once the Klansmen were aligned in two relatively straight columns in the middle of the street, the cross guy dropped his cross. It banged and bounced and broke on the pavement. The crossbar fell off. As the cross guy stooped over to get the broken cross, you could hear him say, "Shit!"

"I guess that's the invocation," I said. "This parade moves too slow."

The cross guy and another Klansman worked for a few seconds to fix the cross by pounding the two pieces together on the pavement. Now that the cross looked even more primitive, with a slanted crossbar, everyone was ready for the parade. The Klansmen began marching down the street, chanting something unintelligible in unison. It sounded as if maybe they practiced being unintelligible together. I should have followed closely along as they marched, but I knew that would place me in danger of eventually understanding something they said. I promised Janice I wouldn't endanger myself, so I lagged far behind them, where all they were was a receding noise.

It didn't look like there was going to be any violence, a blessing that I knew would distress Harmon. As I lagged behind the Klansmen and got up to where Harmon stood on the roof of the building, I stopped to look at him.

"I'm sorry there wasn't any bloodshed," I told him. "I

asked Trollope to have a sniper shoot you. He said the police don't do personal favors."

"Fuck you," Harmon said philosophically.

"Don't flirt with me," I said.

Now it was time to take that bizarre, upsetting event,
evaluate its dozens of details and meanings, throw away
most of the facts, pretend I wasn't human and had no emotions or ideas, then write a pointlessly brief and superficial
narrative from the illusory point of view of someone who
didn't exist: the objective reporter.

I started writing experimental leads on the computer.

Nineteen Ku Klux Klansmen with accordions
and tubas performed James Brown's "I Feel Good"
during an African Unity parade on West Jefferson
Street Saturday.

Dressed in linens purchased at JCPenney White
Sale . . .

Police and State Bureau of Investigation agents
identified all of the Klansmen in Saturday's parade in
downtown St. Beaujolais as known white men.

Riding on a float decorated with 80,000 white
carnations shaped like a shotgun . . .

It was time to look through my notes and hunt
through my mind for a memorable way to start off a story

about the Klan without calling them witless dickheads, which strayed too far from the AP style. I tried it this way:

> Nineteen Ku Klux Klansmen in brilliant white robes and pointed hats began their White Pride parade in downtown St. Beaujolais Saturday by dropping their wooden cross and breaking it on the pavement.
>
> Following repairs to the cross, the Klansmen marched in two columns down West Jefferson Street, fervently chanting something unintelligible to a crowd that barely existed. Police estimated that 30 people watched the Klansmen on their four-block parade. There was no violence, except to the quiet.

# 26

We were sort of fishing, just floating aimlessly far out on the greenish brown water of Baker Lake, a lake named after a famous man no one knew anything about. Bright sunlight shimmered on the water here and there like blinding, liquid mirrors meant only to make us squint away from them. Way above us in the faint blue sky, so faint as if the sun had scorched most of the blue away, a baby thunderhead was trying to be born from a regular cumulonimbus cloud, swelling and puffing around its edges of whiteness so harsh in the sun it made your eyes itch and start to water, looking at where the blurry edges of the cloud in its own shadow seemed to melt into the sky.

Janice knew how to fish and actually had a fishing rod

with a lure on it. She rested the rod under one of her bare thighs, letting the rod lean on the edge of the boat, as if a fish would eventually see the submerged lure and bite on it. I just came along to look at her and talk. I had no practical value.

"How are you doin' at the paper?" she said, opening a can of 7UP for herself.

I knew what she meant. It was like I was on parole from my last offense, being fired, and she wanted to find out if I was healthy and sane or if events were now aligning and accumulating for another purge. I thought she wanted a particular *kind* of answer, one that would comfort her and make her feel safe about me, but I knew I didn't have that kind of answer.

"I'm okay," I said.

"Then you're not okay, if that's all you can say," she said. "Answer me this. Why are you a reporter?"

"I'm not. I'm a writer who got the wrong job," I said, which wasn't going to make either of us feel safe. "It's just like you. You're an archaeologist who works in epidemiology. Not many diseases occur among the dead."

She smiled kind of distractedly, amused but not happy, and said, "Yes. Dead people don't get epidemics."

She lit one of my cigarettes and blew smoke into the air, watching where her fishing line disappeared into the glistening murk. It seemed like I might be down there, too, along with the lure and the invisible fish.

"Sometimes I have no patience with you," she said, not looking at me, watching the disappeared line. "Maybe you *are* a writer who got the wrong job, but you have to keep it. You have no idea where the right one is, or if it'll ever be invented, and so you're this kind of cheerful, ironic renegade, taunting everyone for having their dumb lives and their dumb traditions that can't possibly include you. And do you know what this is like, Kurt? It's like sneering at the only people who can help you because they won't change all of civilization to satisfy your desires."

I felt dizzy and scared, like she was leaving me, or part of her had already left and I just found out. All I could do was quietly be afraid, waiting to see how far she'd left me, even though she was only three feet away and distant enough to make me faint.

She looked at me once, studying my eyes maybe to see if I had enough sense to be scared now, then looked back down into the wavering murk.

"My job isn't what I want either," she said. "I didn't go to college for six years to study archaeology just to be a superfluous woman with a good education that nobody wanted, or one that can barely earn a living. But things simply be*came* that way, Kurt, and it hurt me and angered me, sure. But hell, you have to realize that the whole country isn't just kind of joyously sitting here waiting to provide you with exactly the career you want, and the fucking world doesn't *have* to be fair or even care that you're here. So now I'm studying volumes and volumes of statistics about diseases from people I'll never even see, because it's a job I got and it pays me a living wage and I can drive a car and save money every month and have some simple damn safety that just *I* provide."

The only safety I had was Janice, and it seemed in danger of being suspended now.

"Kurt," she said, holding her hand on her forehead like her head hurt. "This just accumulated in me. I don't mean to sound harsh or mean, like suddenly I'm a bitch. I don't know. Sometimes it hurts me that you have a career and you act like you're just toying with people; like none of life is the way it should be and you're the only one who knows that, so screw everybody and you'll feel what you want and write what you want. Please don't be mad at me for saying this, and if you are, I'm going to have to say too bad, because it's true."

"I'm not mad. I'm dizzy."

"Dizzy?" she said, holding her hand over her eyes like a visor and staring at me in the sun. "Why are you dizzy?"

"It's kind of like you knocked the wind out of me, and I deserved it."

"You do," she said.

"Aren't you going to worry about me?"

"Not yet. I haven't finished knocking the wind out of you. Sometimes I hate my job, too, Kurt, but I don't sneer at everyone at work and tell them to go fuck themselves like you do."

"This is getting serious. Are you going to kill me?"

"I don't want you dead. You won't behave better if you're dead. And now I forgot what I was going to say, dammit," she complained.

"Don't worry. I'm still dizzy."

"You should be."

"I think I'm bleeding internally."

"Good. Bleed some more," she said.

Closing my eyes and leaning my head over quickly with the thought of resting my head on the edge of the boat, my inertia and balance were wrong and I slid head-first into the lake, which I thought Janice would find surprising as I tumbled once underwater and righted myself, pushing to the surface to tread water and look at her.

"Can you swim, can you swim?" she said anxiously, leaning over to reach for me.

"Here?" I said. "I think it's prohibited. They only allow boating and fishing."

When she realized I wasn't drowning, she didn't look scared anymore but just looked puzzled.

"What happened?"

"I fell."

"You just *fell*?"

"Well, it doesn't have to be elaborate, does it? Can't I just fall?" I said, bobbing near the boat.

"You were sitting down. How can you fall when you're sitting down?"

"You mean if I don't explain it right, I fell improperly? Is that it?"

"Are we arguing?"

"No. You're arguing. I'm floating."

"Get back in the boat, Kurt."

"Why? You'll probably criticize the way I floated."

"You're floating just fine."

"You don't mean it. I probably have flaws in my float-ing. Go on. Tell me."

"All right, then. If you're going to be cranky, just float then, and I'll fish," she said, picking up her fishing rod.

"Fine," I said, bobbing precisely where I'd been all the time. "I'm a good floater. Not competitive, really, but ad-equate. My shoes are getting heavy, though."

"Don't go near my hook."

"You sure are bossy today."

"Let's not argue. We came out here to relax."

"I'm relaxing. Floating makes me feel calm."

"You look calm. I'm going to read my book now," she said, reaching into her bag and pulling out a paperback. She rested the fishing rod on her leg and opened the book.

"What book is it?" I asked, making wide sweeps in the water with my arms.

"*Love in the Time of Cholera*," she said.

"Oh," I said, nodding my head. "I didn't bring a book."

"I know."

I let her read for a while, for about thirty seconds.

"Janice?"

"Yes."

"I'm getting lonesome. Will you read to me?"

"You have to get in the boat first."

"I hope we're not fighting anymore. Are we?"

"If we are, I have the advantage," she said. "I have a boat."

"I know. It's a nice boat. I wish *I* had a boat."

"Aren't you getting tired?" she said, putting the book down.

"And sleepy, too. I'd take a nap, but I'd sink."

"Give me your hand," she said as she reached for me.

"I'll give you the rest of me, too, unless it's just the hand you want," I said, as we grabbed each other's fingers and she began pulling me in.

# 27

On the day the Small Board of Aldermen was scheduled to vote on hiring Dalton Donner as the town's police chief, members of the First, Second, and possibly Third Baptist churches assembled in front of town hall with pious anger and posters warning against Sodom and Gomorrah. Sallie Hind from the *Journal* was there, interviewing some woman and asking the predictable, dumb questions in utter seriousness.

"As a Christian, do you regard homosexuality as a sin?" she asked the woman as I stood nearby. It made me think of saying "Excuse me, ma'am. Is the Baptist church opposed to both oral sex and written sex?"

Camera crews and reporters from two TV stations ran

around peevishly trying to tape interviews without getting members of the enemy TV station in their shots. When one of the camera guys realized I was a reporter and I didn't look like an outraged Baptist, he didn't want me in the background as he prepared to tape an interview.

"Would you move?" he said, waving me away with his hand.

I shook my head no, and discreetly gave him the finger. Instead of leaving me alone, which would have been sensible, he walked up to me with an angry expression and said quietly, "We're taping an interview, asshole. Move out of the shot."

He wasn't much bigger than me, and I lifted weights, so I didn't move.

"Shove your camera up your ass. You could call it a medical feature," I said.

He decided then that I was part of the background, and he left me alone. I didn't want to be on TV with a bunch of outraged Christians anyway, so I walked out of the shot and roamed across the town-hall lawn, searching for whoever appeared to be the least pissed-off Christian to interview. Talking with morally outraged people was a painful indignity. They had a tendency to assume that if you didn't appear to be as angry and sickened as they were, you were probably one of the people they despised, or you soon would be. I saw an old woman with white hair and, instead of an expression of holy wrath made worse from all of this public attention, a fairly calm, aloof look on her face. She looked safe to interview, so I walked up to her and politely introduced myself, asking what she hoped to accomplish in the protest.

"Well," she said, leaning her Sodom and Gomorrah poster away from her head, "as devoted servants of the Lord, we need to keep the queers out of Small. Let 'em work in St. Beaujolais, where they already is."

I wrote that down in my notepad, but there was a style problem.

"I'm not sure if I can use that quote, ma'am," I said. "I don't think we say 'queers' in our newspaper. Could you say 'gays'?"

"Queers is queers," she said, looking up at me with suspicion.

"Yes, ma'am, and roses is roses. But to overcome this style problem, it would be helpful if you either said gay or homosexual."

"I don't see why I have to be helpful," she said. "Queers is queers."

This wasn't working, so I digressed. Pointing at her poster, which said, "No Sodom and Gomorrah in Small!," I said, "I think the only way you could get Sodom and Gomorrah in Small is to annex Israel. I don't think the aldermen have the authority to annex a foreign nation."

It was a good digression, and bewildered the woman enough that she looked away and pretended I wasn't there.

But I couldn't go back to the bureau and tell Lisa I succeeded in making everyone pretend I wasn't there. Unfortunately I had to interview somebody and get a fresh portion of their anger or hatred or fear. Nearby on the sidewalk was a fat man in a brown suit carrying a poster saying, "The Lord will destroy this city," a Biblical quote the poster said was in chapter 19, verse 14 of Genesis. Trying to appear interested but neutral, I walked up to the man, told him who I was, and said, "That quote, on your poster. Is that a reference to Sodom or Gomorrah?" All I meant was it had to be one city or the other, and I wanted to know which one.

"It's a reference to Small," the man said, looking at me with indignation or something like it.

"Small?" I said, taking notes. "I didn't know Small was in the Bible. This really *is* an old town, isn't it?"

My lightness was a severe burden on the man, who scowled at me and held up a black copy of the Bible, which he pointed at me like a weapon.

"Small is *not* in the book of Genesis," he said irritably. "If you knew anything at *all* about the Bible, which I don't expect out of the left-leaning liberal media, you'd know it refers to Judea."

Nothing was going to work. Irony and intelligence were alien forces to these people, and I was the alien general. Shielding myself with politeness, I said, "Sir, I know Small isn't mentioned in the Bible. It's just that when you said the quote on your poster referred to Small, that would mean, literally, that Small is named in Genesis, which we both know isn't true."

"Well, then quit saying it is," the man said, refusing to grasp anything I said. Opening his Bible to chapter 19, verse 14 of Genesis, he showed me the quote.

"Does it say Small?" he asked.

I wanted to grab him around his head and fling him to the sidewalk. Instead, I acted like I was reading the Bible.

"No. It doesn't say Small there," I said. "I guess North Carolina is mentioned in one of the later chapters. Thank you for your instruction."

I walked away before he got any madder. That afternoon at my apartment, I got out my paperback copy of the King James version of the Bible to look through chapter 19 of Genesis again and found something surpassingly weird. It alluded to homosexuality, or at least *some* kind of sexual sin, saying the Lord destroyed Sodom and Gomorrah with brimstone and fire because of those sins. Lot escaped. And then, a few verses later in the same chapter, there was more sex. Two nights in a row, Lot's two daughters got him drunk on wine and copulated with him.

"Thus were both the daughters of Lot with child by their father," the Bible said.

In the same chapter, then, two cities were destroyed because of sexual sins, and two women received no punishment for copulating with their drunken father. Somehow, I was going to get that in the morning paper.

# 28

It was the largest unwanted triumph of my career in newspapers when my story came out and I was accused of irreverence for quoting scripture. The people least capable of understanding irony were the ones creating all of it. Seven people called the bureau, either to revile me personally or to ask Lisa to revile me, which she wouldn't do.

"They all want a retraction," Lisa said as we talked in her office.

"They want us to apologize for correctly describing the Bible," I said.

She nodded her head and looked astonished. "I can't imagine why this should be happening," she said.

"It's too weird. I like it," I said as Rebecca walked up

to the doorway and said Andrew Christopher was on the phone for me. Lisa handed me her phone and stared at me like a girl waiting to see if someone else was going to get punished.

"Hello," I said.

"Kurt," Christopher said.

"Andrew," I said.

"What the fuck are you people doin' in St. Beaujolais? Destroying all of Christianity?"

"I don't think we have enough people for that."

"I'm glad. I've already had three calls from enraged people in Small this morning sayin' you blasphemed the Bible by quoting scripture."

We both were silent there, wondering what could possibly be said next.

"Yes," I said. "Did you read the story?"

"Of course I did. It says the aldermen voted to hire a prominent Colorado homosexual as police chief. It says some Baptists in Small don't think homosexuals should be hired for anything. And then you quote Genesis, sayin' Sodom and Gomorrah were destroyed for sexual sins and a drunken old man had sex with his daughters."

There was silence again. I sipped some Coke and lit a cigarette.

"Did you verify that?" Christopher said in a serious tone that I knew wasn't serious.

"You mean the Bible?" I said.

"Yes."

"No. I admit I didn't verify the Bible."

Christopher coughed briefly. He said, "So. We printed unverified information."

"Yes. We did."

"Well then, do you think we should run a retraction?"

"You mean, apologize to the public for quoting scripture, because we don't have any witnesses or court documents saying Lot had sex with his daughters because they got him drunk?"

"Yes," Christopher said. "Should we run a retraction saying we don't know if the Bible's a reliable document?"

"That would be fun."

"Too much fun."

"Well, we could run a clarification," I suggested.

"Saying what?"

"Saying because the *News-Dispatch* was unable to verify events that happened a few thousand years ago in Palestine, our reporters aren't responsible for the content of the Bible."

"Type it up, Kurt," he said. "Keep it short. Send it to me by five."

I hung up before either of us could change our minds. Such a clarification was to me more precious than most stories I'd ever written. It represented humanity and absurdity in a dangerously pure form, and I admired it and was grateful that Christopher and I had been in precisely the right moods to envision the minor greatness of apologizing to the public for the troubling existence of scripture. And so it came to pass that this was printed the next morning in the paper:

> Clarification: The *News-Dispatch* regrets that some readers of a religious bent might find this paper irresponsible for a statement made in an article in yesterday's edition that Lot's two daughters took turns getting him drunk and engaging in sexual acts with him. Our authority for the statement was *Genesis 19:32–37, Holy Bible,* Authorized Version, known as the "King James Translation." In the absence of corroborative historical documentation for the event—which occurred approximately 2,000 years prior to the date of the King James translation—we hope that our readers will accept both that statement as well as others cited in the same article concerning the destruction of the cities of Sodom and Gomorrah (*Gen.* 18:20–33, 19:1–5) and the turning of Lot's wife into a pillar of salt (*Gen.* 19:26) as having been made in good faith by the translators of the Authorized Version, in accordance with the evidence available to them at the time.

You could never be sure, really, what overall effect this had on the reading public. But in our bureau, we liked to believe we could have won a Nobel Prize for clarifications.

And Chief Donner liked it. Having never spoken with me before except over the phone, Donner and I met at the Crystal Palace Bar & Grill two nights after his employment was confirmed by the aldermen, and Donner was just studying the night life in his new town and meeting people at the Crystal Palace. I was there with Janice.

Donner sipped a glass of National Bohemian beer and thanked me for my recent story that kind of gently satirized people for using the Bible to condemn homosexuality while ignoring Lot's daughters screwing their father. Sitting at the bar next to me and Janice, Donner said, "Usually when I deal with the press, I get scrutinized, analyzed, and victimized. So I have to admit I was pleasantly astonished to see your article about the little protests, and also that unusual clarification."

"I don't think clarification is the word," Janice said. "I think 'taunt' is the word."

"I like to taunt the readers," I said.

"Yes, and they'll nail you someday for it," Janice said.

"I don't know about taunts, but I personally enjoyed it," Donner said.

"Well, I hate to sound selfish, but I didn't do it for you," I said. "I did it for me. I just thought it was unfair for people to pretend that scripture justified their anger and hatred when they were plainly ignoring another part of the scripture showing a drunken man having sex with his daughters, as if that were fine."

"Most newspapers wouldn't *print* such a contrast, even if it *is* plainly in the Bible," Donner said. "Is your paper different?"

Janice shook her head, saying, "No. But Kurt sure as hell is. You never can tell who he'll outrage next."

# 29

The next curious thing that happened was that an angry and kind of horrified woman called the bureau to announce that she and several other parents were filing complaints of child abuse against an employee of a kindergarten who tried disciplining the children by saying she'd suck their brains from their ears if they weren't quiet. I wondered if this was similar to eating crawdads in New Orleans. I'd seen people suck the brains out of crawdads before, but I didn't know if there was a Cajun recipe for kindergarteners.

"My four-year-old son came home from the Five Ducks Kindergarten and told me that Miss Beasley at the school had threatened to suck the childrens' brains from their ears if they didn't stop making noise and behave themselves," the woman said in an agitated and somewhat angry voice over the phone. I couldn't imagine any proper way to react to what I'd just been told.

"Did the woman suck anyone's ears?" I said, deciding not to ask the woman if her son still had his brain.

"As far as I know she didn't, but we still regard it as assault for a grown adult telling harmless children that she'll suck their brains through their ears. And we've called the district attorney's office to seek criminal charges."

I called Susan Crewes, the district attorney, trying to pose my questions to her tersely and with vast disinterest.

"Is it illegal to tell children you'll suck their brains out?" I said.

"Off the record, Kurt, I don't think you could. Their ears are too small," she said.

"Well, if you *attempted* to suck their brains out, even though you knew it wasn't possible, is it illegal?"

"Are you really doing a serious news story on this?" she asked.

"Sure we are. You're taught in journalism school that it's always news if people threaten to suck your internal organs."

"They actually teach that?"

"I wouldn't know. I studied English."

"I don't know why you're trying to make a big deal out of this, Kurt."

"I know. Brain-sucking is so ordinary. I hate the press, don't you?"

"You despise your own profession?"

"I could despise yours, too, if it makes me seem more broad-minded."

Looking for more balance or thoroughness in the story, I called the head of the university medical school for professional views.

"Even if you could generate enough suction through the human mouth to make a brain move, which I can't imagine is possible," he said, "it's reasonable to argue that the ear is too small an orifice to allow for the passage of a relatively bulky organ like a brain."

"That's what I thought," I said.

"Was it necessary to call a physician to confirm an obvious opinion?" the head wanted to know.

"In journalism it is. Reporters are ordered to make believe that their own intelligence and common sense don't matter unless it's gained in an interview with someone else. In other words, editors wouldn't dare allow me to simply say in this story that it's probably impossible to suck a child's brain through his ear, even though no one would argue with that, because reporters aren't supposed to put *their* opinions in a story. So you need an authority to state the obvious."

"I'm not an authority," he said. "As far as I know, no one's an authority on brain-sucking."

"Wow. It's a whole new field. Should I call the Department of Brain-Sucking at Johns Hopkins?"

"I wasn't aware they had one."

"I wonder if it's in the Yellow Pages."

Eventually I had to end this systematic interviewing
and take my story notes down the street to Stanley's where
I sat by myself on the deathly humid terrace while drinking
Central American coffee from a nation we hadn't invaded
yet as I experimented on my legal pad with straightforward, perplexing ways to write this newest news for the
morning paper. People who thought life in St. Beaujolais
and Small was relatively civil and refined might open the
paper to read this sentence:

> Threats to suck kindergarteners' brains through
> their ears are being examined tentatively by the dis-
> trict attorney.

It seemed too fantastical to be true, while the main
quality it had was that of being true. Sometimes if you just
wrote the truth without exaggeration, no one would believe
it. Then I began to wonder if you could say "suck" in a
family paper, such as "suck on this, this sucks, go suck a
dead dog." This wasn't particularly helpful for my story,
but I knew a lot of people disliked the word "suck" and
might find it offensive in the news. Was there a genteel way
to discuss brain-sucking? Probably Miss Manners knew.

On my legal pad I wrote:

>   Although a University physician says brain-sucking isn't a credible skill, the Vermilion-Wellington County district attorney is investigating a reported threat to suck kindergarteners' brains through their ears.

In a way, it didn't seem possible or even advisable to correctly write this story as if I were alerting the public to the horrors of something that almost certainly wasn't a real threat. My general usefulness to the public was under suspicion again, but that was a truth about journalism anyway. Sometimes the news wasn't worth knowing, but like a child picking up a handful of exotic, unidentified crud from the bottom of a ditch, we carried it home, just in case.

As I glanced up from my private, journalistic ditch, there was Janice, and some old man with her, staring at me from the end of the terrace and walking down the little aisle toward me.

"Hey," I said, because that was how people were supposed to greet each other in this part of the South. In Kansas City, people said "Hi," but I'd learned in North Carolina that you talked like you came from the "Andy Griffith Show." So if I'd been sitting there on the terrace at Stanley's and Pope John Paul II approached me with a bunch of cardinals and bishops, I wouldn't say, "Good evening, your holiness." I'd say, "Hey, your holiness."

"Hey," Janice said back to me as she and the old man arrived at my table. "Kurt, this is my father, Joseph."

I stood up abruptly to shake his hand.

"We came here for an early dinner," Janice said as she put her arm around my waist. "Daddy flew in from Philadelphia today, and I'm so glad we ran into you here. Are you working on a story here? Well, Daddy, you get to see a newspaper story being written for the morning paper."

"Well, please have a seat," I said.

"We can't interrupt your work," Mr. Galassi said.

"Yes, you can. It's not hard," I said. "Please, go on and have a seat. I'll finish the story later."

"Let me see your lead," Janice said, taking my legal pad and holding it up in front of her.

"Those are just notes. I'm still working on it," I said.

"What's it about?" Mr. Galassi said. Before I could explain or object, Janice started reading aloud from my notes.

"Threats to suck kindergarteners' brains through their ears are being examined tentatively by the district attorney," Janice read, sniggering and putting the notes down to stare at me with amusement and maybe some embarrassment that she had no idea what this meant but she'd just read it in front of her father, who probably couldn't imagine I was a serious, responsible reporter if I sat at a table at Stanley's writing bizarre descriptions of brainsucking.

"What's *that* all about?" Mr. Galassi said wonderingly.

"Yeah, Kurt. Is there some Satanic cult at a *kinder*-garten?" Janice asked.

"I think that would go on the religion page. That's not

my beat," I said, taking my notes from Janice so I wouldn't
have to explain them right then.

Mr. Galassi smiled at me and said, "So *you're* the young
man Janice has been telling me about."

"I hope so. I hope she hasn't been telling you about
some other man," I said.

"I was, but he insisted on hearing about you, so I told
him," Janice said.

"Actually, you're almost the only person she talked
about," Mr. Galassi said.

"I told her I'd give her a dollar if she did that," I said,
pulling out my wallet and getting a dollar out. Janice
smiled and took the dollar.

"He doesn't pay very well, does he?" Mr. Galassi said.

"No, but he's a nice man," Janice said. "He doesn't
earn much now because he's a journalist, but he can give
me more money for saying nice things about him when he
sells a southern novel he's writing called *Uncle Tom's Cabin
Cruiser.*"

I'd forgotten about that. Across the table, Janice
grinned at me.

"Uncle Tom's *Cabin Cruiser*?" Mr. Galassi said.

I nodded my head. "Yeah. One night while Janice and
I were barbecuing some chicken and talking about what
we hoped to do in life, I was rambling about important
southern novels written by Northerners and decided inex-
cusably to write a novel called *Uncle Tom's Cabin Cruiser.* It

would be about a slave working for the Securities and Exchange Commission. That's how he can afford the boat."

"The Securities and Exchange Commission? You didn't give him that job when we first talked about it," Janice said.

"A lot of time has passed. I promoted him."

# 30

It was Janice's idea to take her father, who was a sixty-two-year-old retired police detective, down to The Tomb with its clientele dressed variously for the tastes of a rock club, a redneck bar, or a jail.

"This is like descending into hell," Mr. Galassi said as he stared at the low-hanging, fake rock ceiling and the fake rock walls protruding jaggedly everywhere in a steady haze of cigarette smoke, like the imagined dimness of hell.

"Hell doesn't have Christmas lights," Janice said, pointing at the string of tiny Christmas lights suspended from the ceiling.

"By God," Mr. Galassi said, as if discovering another unexpected weirdness. "This is *July*."

"They have July in hell," Janice said.

"Do they? I wonder what winter is like in hell. Do they have molten snow?" I said.

"This place reminds me of jail," Mr. Galassi said.

"We wanted you to feel at home, Daddy," Janice said.

"Then I should be questioning a robbery or murder suspect," he said.

"We'll introduce you to some of them later," I said. "First let me get you and Janice a beer." I got them each a bottle of Rolling Rock, and Mr. Galassi stared curiously, maybe even suspiciously, at my bottle of Soho Cream Soda.

"Isn't that a childrens' drink?" he said, sounding like a detective. "You're not much of a drinker."

From the corner of my eye I saw Janice blink or flinch, and almost imperceptibly, I felt her fingers in the middle of my back, as if to protect me. I wondered how you conversationally said you're an alcoholic and you don't want to painfully deteriorate, watch your mind vanish, and die.

"Actually I'm an excellent drinker," I said, reaching behind me to put my finger in Janice's hand. She grasped my finger. "I could probably drink more than anybody in this room and not even feel sleepy. But once you get that good, excellence becomes lethal. So when I realized I'd mastered everything that matters about drinking, I quit."

Mr. Galassi looked a little embarrassed, as if realizing I'd been accidentally cornered and, out of politeness to myself, I wasn't going to say I was an alcoholic.

"Oh, *oh*," he said, kind of apologetically. "So you're on the *wagon*?"

"I wonder why people always think of a wagon," I said, "as if, if you don't drink, you're expected to get on this particular wagon. And it's always *the* wagon, implying that of the hundreds of thousands of people in the world who quit drinking, all of them somehow are crushed and smashed and gathered simultaneously on just one wagon."

"So you're *not* on the wagon," Mr. Galassi said.

"I hate that expression. It makes me envision alcoholics on a hayride," I said, smiling slightly. "Like people spending the summer at Camp Detox. Everyone get on the wagon, now. We're gonna drive this son of a bitch at full speed and see how many of you fall off. Uh-oh. A bump. Ahhhhhhh! Well, there went *some* of 'em. At Camp Detox, we're looking for the few, the proud: Alcoholics on a Hayride. And do you know what I just realized? The acronym for Alcoholics on a Hayride would be this: Ahhhhh!"

# 31

The following day at work, in one of my ordinary seizures of severe and chronic whimsy, I devised a new rule of English: "i before e except on Friday."

This came after Marta was trying to spell "seize" in a story she was doing about cops seizing some marijuana. On her computer she had written "The officers siezed approximately 50 bags of marijuana."

"This doesn't look right. How do you spell seize?" she said.

"I don't," I said.

"But if you use the rule 'i before e except after c,' then I've spelled it right," she said. "But it still doesn't look right."

I got out my dictionary and saw that it was spelled with the e before the i.

"The old rule doesn't apply," I said. "Because today's Friday, the new rule is 'i before e except on Friday.'"

"Thank you, Kurt. You're unbearably helpful," Marta said.

Distractedly, because that's all I was good at then, I wondered about doing a follow-up on the kindergarten story, saying no charges could be filed because the district attorney saw no genuine criminal threat in telling children you were going to suck their brains through their ears. It was rude, but not criminal. First, I distractedly studied Perrault's new memo:

> Reporters invariably deal with sensitive, upsetting subjects in the community, such as rape; incest; child abuse; pederasty; sex with farm animals; prominent homosexuals; Satanism; lesbians who want sperm; property taxes; and cock fighting. Always we need to exercise our utmost care and prudence in selecting a story that's newsworthy and in writing that story in a way that's both factual, balanced, correct, responsible, tasteful, and follows the basic tenets of sound newswriting.
>
> Sometimes a reporter, aided by an inattentive editor, deviates from sound journalism, as in the recent story on the unfortunate children in St. Beaujolais

who were led to believe that their kindergarten teacher would suck their brains out. Doubtless, the story was somewhat newsworthy, since an apparent threat against innocent children was made. But in my experienced view, the lead of the story placed too much emphasis on brain-sucking and failed to name a specific, tenable criminal offense in a more abstract manner, such as assault. The reporter also might have been taking liberties in his writing style by inserting fatuous information from a neurologist announcing the slight likelihood of anyone sucking out a child's brain.

The story could have been far more precise and readable had the reporter simply stated the basic facts and avoided extraneous musings and implied humor about something so serious as a child's brain. Perhaps we need to re-examine our mission to provide the public with concise, unadorned facts that aren't wantonly interpreted by unmindful reporters.

Normally you could ignore Perrault's memos. I'd been told to regard him as a pompous figurehead, a former reporter and editor who, if he ever had much extraordinary skill in journalism, found no occasion to display it anymore. His advice was never wanted and was followed—if at all—begrudgingly. While he sat in his distant office in Hampton, drawing an unknown salary to match his concealed worth, other editors actually ran the paper, and Perrault fired memos at everyone like a retired general fucking around with the artillery and striking his own troops. His newest memo was far longer than normal, and instead of blathering tediously about his latest annoyance and then shutting up, he seemed to have found a more volatile source for his suspicion and hostility. Me.

Everyone else in the bureau told me to ignore the memo anyway, like I always did.

"Maybe you should go to Hampton and suck his brain through his ears," Harmon said.

"I wonder why he suddenly doesn't like me," I said. "I've been trying to write in my style and violate every tradition he believes in for about two months. Is he just now noticing?"

"Could be," Rebecca speculated. "Or maybe somebody complained about your story, and Perrault, who otherwise doesn't notice anything, was forced to realize you exist."

"Could we tell him to stop reading the paper?" I wondered. "I know what. I'll send him a memo saying what his staff writes is none of his business."

# 32

My story in the morning paper, which I assumed at least several thousand people read for their general well-being, said, "Criminal charges won't be filed against a woman who said she would suck the brains out of kinder-garteners' ears because brain-sucking can't be regarded as a credible threat, District Attorney Susan Crewes said Friday."

I liked it. It was true, concise, and exceedingly strange. Lisa worried about my prose style, though. She said I could have written a more harmless lead such as "District Attorney Susan Crewes says no basis exists for filing criminal charges against a St. Beaujolais kindergarten teacher who threatened a bizarre punishment for noisy children."

"Child abuse is a sensitive issue, Kurt," she said as we talked in her office.

"You mean *brain*-sucking is a sensitive issue," I said. "Although how do we know? It's never happened before, so no one has any opinions on it. I know what you really mean. You don't like my lead because it faithfully repeats the grotesque threat of sucking children's brains out, as if we're supposed to report the truth without *saying* the truth because it's upsetting. If my writing style is upsetting it's because the world is upsetting."

She didn't particularly want to say I was right.

"I could have rewritten your lead if I'd wanted to," she said.

"Yes, and thank you for not doing it."

"Why can't you be a normal reporter and write serious, straightforward, abstract crap that doesn't show any trace of irony or comprehension of how strange your job is?"

"I'm not that way."

"Why can't you just be an ordinary, muck-raking reporter who wants to tell the truth in a highly imitative style that's indistinguishable from the style of ten thousand other reporters?"

"Being ordinary is a disease."

"Would it kill you to write like everyone else and be a dutiful AP clone?"

"I don't know. I'll never do it."

"Well, here's something to think about," she said. "Perrault."

"What about Perrault?"

"I'll tell you about Perrault. Everyone thinks he's just this harmless old man remote from everything and pleasantly unable to have an effect on the paper anymore, but I don't know. He still has the luxury of power, and you've pissed him off."

"I know. I worry about that. Do you think he'll do anything other than remain pissed off and write snotty memos?"

"Well, it's not something I'm going to *ask* him, Kurt. But what I worry about for you is that Perrault, like most editors, is pretty much an orthodox traditionalist. That is, he thinks *all* stories should be written however it was he got used to writing them him*self* back whenever it was that he was most successful and started getting promoted. I don't know what most journalism schools are teaching now, or what they taught when Perrault was a student, but a basic axiom that I don't think will ever be changed is that, in fact, I think the axiom was in one of your notes on the bulletin board: Dare to be the same. I'm pretty damn sure that Perrault honors that axiom, and when someone like *you* comes along, defying the great sameness of the world and sneering at every tradition, he's going to want to kick your ass, you know."

"I know."

We sat quietly for a few seconds, as if allowing me to be noiselessly in trouble and begin wondering how I might change myself to become ordinary. It would never happen.

# 33

A meeting was held in the bureau to discuss the newspaper's policy on shit.

"You've seen this," Lisa said to everyone, holding a copy of Perrault's newest memo.

"Oh shit," Harmon said. When he was interviewing a university student about attitudes toward the role of the military in achieving a president's political goals, Harmon asked why the student felt it was fine for George Bush to send twenty-some-thousand soldiers to Panama and over-throw a government. The student's answer, which got printed in the paper, was: "Sometimes the greatest good for the greatest number is achieved by kicking the shit out of someone." We did get a few disagreeable phone calls from incensed readers who wouldn't say "shit" over the phone, and we were too polite to say "shit" either, so we just had to guess that shit was the subject they so despised in the paper. Perrault despised it, too. His memo said: "There plainly has been some uncertainty among our staff on the *News-Dispatch*'s policy about vulgarities and obscenities. This is our policy: Don't use them.

"The definition of a family paper is one that contains reading matter suitable for a prude, and that's who you should assume you're writing for: a prude."

"We're just writing for one person?" I said. "We need more subscribers than that."

"It doesn't matter how many liberals in Vermilion County read communist homosexual novels written by gay lesbians who think the s word is a commonplace expression," the memo said. "Other papers can wallow in the s word if they want to. Ours won't."

"Is the policy clear?" Lisa said wearily.

"If you're interviewing Miss Manners and she says shit, can you use it?" Harmon said.

"You probably won't be interviewing Miss Manners," Lisa said.

Theresa raised her hand and said, "I have a question. Kurt asked me to ask if we're just writing for one prude, could you tell us what his name is so we could refer to him by name in all of our stories? I'll bet it begins with an *s*."

"If you have any further questions, write them down

on a piece of paper and save it until you forget you have it," Lisa said, turning and walking indifferently toward her office. The meeting was over.

"Let's go across the street and have a beer," Theresa said, looking at Harmon and me.

"Okay, but no more than three or four. I'm watching my weight," Harmon said.

"Other people are watching your weight, too," I said.

"Eat me."

"I don't eat pork."

Harmon raised a fist toward my face, playfully, it seemed. "Someday I'm gonna kick your ass."

"You couldn't raise your foot that far," I said.

"Don't fight in the bureau. Go to Stanley's and do it," Theresa said.

Across the street after Theresa and Harmon ordered their beers and I ordered a Coke, Harmon said, "I don't think I've ever seen you drink a beer or wine or bourbon or anything traditionally associated with this dissolute profession."

"*All* reporters drink," Theresa said in her girlish, mocking voice. "You'll ruin our reputations if people see you at the bar drinking a Coke."

It was terrible when people didn't know they were cheerfully hurting you. And to tell them would only hurt you more.

"I already had some dry sherry," I said.

"Today?" Theresa said.

"Five months ago," I said. "I quit drinking sherry because it begins with an *s*. And then I quit drinking altogether. I don't drink any alcohol with vowels or consonants in it."

"Good Lord," Theresa said with amazement or something. "How can you go for five months without a drink?"

I wanted to know that, too.

"It's not good to stay sober too long," Harmon said. "Sober begins with an *s*, too."

Please be quiet.

"Do you drink at all?" Theresa said in a simply curious tone.

I shook my head no and said, "Like a gila monster, I get all my liquids from eating reptiles and rodents."

"*Stop* it," she said.

"I guess you don't like zoology," I said, sipping my Coke. "I see why you wouldn't. We work for one of the biggest reptiles in the business: Perrault. He's not really a reptile, though. He's a dick. That's a different phylum."

"Speaking of Perrault," Harmon said, "it's your fault we're getting all these snotty memos now. He never cared about anything until you came here and started pissing him off. He used to just write memos that had nothing to *do* with anything we wrote. But now I'm afraid he's actually reading our stories."

"I think you're right," Theresa said. "It seems like all

his memos used to just be these sort of remote little things about journalism in general, like the time he told us to always double-check our spelling of the names of Chinese Communist officials, even though we never write about Chinese Communist officials. But since *you've* been here," she said, looking at me, "all his memos seem kind of harshly directed at whatever we do."

"Whatever *I* do," I said. "Why does he need me for an enemy if he never needed one before?"

Theresa smiled with her eyes wide open. "Well, Kurt, he never needed an enemy before because you weren't available."

# 34

Sometimes I was a snarling wolverine of the free press, prepared to reveal troubling developments in society that I kept learning no one really cared about, such as The Next Estate.

The Next Estate was a happy project in the wilderness of Wellington County in which happy developers purchased more than seven hundred acres on which they would build an enormously expensive eighteen-hole golf course designed by Jack Nicklaus. Splayed out around the golf course, within the ancient, hardwood forests, would be more than eight hundred condominiums and private homes. The cheap residences would cost about three hundred thousand dollars or more. The bigger ones would cost around half a million dollars or a lot more. People who lived there would be a homogeneous social group known as the wealthy but more emphatically as the really goddamn rich. Some of them probably would buy a condominium or a house to stay there just for a day or two at a time so they'd have a charming place to stay while they were in the area to watch a football or basketball game at the university. Along the entire perimeter of The Next Estate would be a wall or fence of some sort, and the entrance gate to the community would be constantly watched by uniformed guards to keep out distressingly unfortunate creatures such as myself. Not long after The Next Estate was started and it was the duty of the press to write about it, my project was to write a series of leads that I knew wouldn't be printed. One lead was "More than three centuries after Europeans moved to America to escape the oppression of an autocratic society ruled by the rich and elite, The Next Estate is being built near St. Beaujolais as a sanctuary for the rich and elite."

It was automatically rejected.

"We can't print that. It's true," Lisa told me.

I tried an alternate lead: "With a wall around it to keep out blacks, Hispanics, Indians, and newspaper reporters, The Next Estate golfing community is being built by the U.S. Game & Wildlife Commission as a preserve for rich old white people."

Eventually it was announced by state archaeologists

that hundreds if not thousands of artifacts from prehistoric Indians probably lay buried on parts of The Next Estate land. While this was extremely interesting to the archaeologists, no state law compelled the owners of private property to look for Indian artifacts on their land, so it was a certainty that whatever artifacts were there would be soon covered up forever by a Jack Nicklaus golf course and about a thousand buildings.

"Pricks," Janice said as she brooded about that news. "Why doesn't anybody ever care about the Indians?"

"Because you're not supposed to care about the people you stole a continent from," I said.

"Well, *we* do, and we're going there," she said of us.

"Going where?"

"The Next Estate. We're going to drive out there and hike around."

"You mean trespass?"

"I don't care. This whole nation was based on a theft from the Indians," she said, walking into the bedroom to put on her hiking boots. "Now they're going to put their exclusive, elegant homes and their eighteen-goddamn-hole golf course out in a private, rich-guy sanctuary right on *top* of where prehistoric Indians used to wander. Well, I want to *see* it before it's destroyed and whitenized and turned into a forbidden, vulgar golf preserve, as if a bunch of fat old golfers losing their balls on a fairway is culturally and historically superior to the ancient people who wandered here thousands of years before Europeans sailed over and said to the Indians, 'We're going to steal this country and play golf.'"

As Janice put on her hiking clothes, I asked if we should bring the Beretta with us. If we saw a herd of golfers, we could shoot some and sell their pelts. She said leave the gun home.

And so it came to pass that we drove on out to The Next Estate, parking her car along a rutted dirt road remote from where the construction crews traveled, and we began walking along some animal trail surrounded everywhere by pines and oaks and huge trees whose names we didn't know, as well as a constant supply of flying bugs that bumped into us.

"What if someone asks us what we're doing here?" Janice said.

"Are you worried about trespassing now? You weren't earlier," I said. "If anyone spots us and yells, 'Hey! What're you doin' here,' I'll just say 'We're rich white people. Fuck you.'"

"It might work," Janice said. "But what if they ask why rich white people are wandering around in the woods with bugs all over them?"

"Well, they shouldn't ask that. If rich white people want to act eccentric and irrational from years of having sex with their cousins and sisters, it's their privilege."

We walked along a creek to look for artifacts because

Janice said Indians would have lived and hunted near a source of fresh water.

"Although," she said, "they could've lived anywhere and this creek might not even have existed when Indians were here, so it almost doesn't matter *where* we look. Except if we look in the trees, we'll step all over copperheads. Although copperheads could be anywhere, and we might step on them anyway. So the best place to look for artifacts is anywhere."

"Oh. We're being methodical," I said.

"Don't make fun of me, Kurt."

"I'm not. You go over there and look anywhere, and I'll go over here and look anywhere. And look. I already found something. A skink."

"We don't want skinks."

"Skinks are neat. See his metallic blue tail? Why do skinks need metallic blue tails? It can't be camouflage, unless they're going to hide in an art-supply store."

"We're looking for arrowheads and spearheads," Janice said as we slowly walked along the creek bank, squinting down at moss and weeds and thousands of pieces of decaying plants layered all over the rocky ground.

"And golf balls," I said.

"Prehistoric Indians didn't play golf, I don't think."

"How do you know?"

"Because we've never found any Indian burial grounds with golf clubs in them," she said, looking up to smile at me with her lovely dark eyes and stare at me for a while.

"Will we be famous," I said as we slowly walked, "if we find a prehistoric golfing tribe?"

"Infinitely. But we're not likely to find any bones. And if we do, it's more likely to be a deer than an Indian."

"We could do a Piltdown golfing Indian, you know," I said as I squatted next to Janice and watched her pick up some little black stones from the creek.

"What's that?" she said in a doubtful tone.

"Those are little black rocks. *You* picked them up."

"No. I mean what's a Piltdown golfing Indian? Some fraudulent project of yours?"

"Yeah, like the phony discovery at Piltdown, England. We could get some old bones and a round, black rock and say it was a golf ball. Then we'd take the bones and the rock to the university and say, 'My God. We've found the remains of a Paleolithic golfer out at The Next Estate.'"

"Okay," Janice said cheerfully. "You find some old bones. I'll look here in the creek for a ten-thousand-year-old golf ball. What will we *name* the tribe?"

"I don't have a name."

"All discoverers get to name their discoveries. You'll have to think of a name for the tribe."

"The Nicklai," I said. "An ancient Indian tribe named after Jack Nicklaus."

"That's a good one. We'll use it. Have you found any old bones yet?"

"I'm still looking."

"Here. I think I found a primitive golfing tee older than the Assyrian Empire. No. It's just a rock," she said, smiling and throwing it back in the creek.

"Janice? What's that? The skeletal remains of an Indian caddie born before Christ?" I said, pointing across the creek. "No. It's just a pine tree."

I had to go back to the bureau that afternoon, a Saturday, and do a Sunday piece about Indians and golf and The Next Estate. It wasn't, to me, just a routine, abstract matter of telling the indifferent public that some archaeologists were complaining that some old stones and bones belonging to vanished humans could be damaged or covered up forever because wealthy people wanted to golf in haughty seclusion. I tried to write it with the kind of personal insight and attitude that I sensed was most appropriate to that small fragment of the reading public most likely to care what I wrote: me.

Janice got the paper from the yard late Sunday morning and brought it to bed where we could sit together and see if what I wrote got printed. It did. It started off:

State archaeologist Gerald Litner said the prehistoric Indians who once wandered where The Next

Estate golfing community is being built might as well be named the Nicklai Indians, after Jack Nicklaus.

"Since we don't know who the Indians were," Litner said Saturday, "and many of their artifacts are likely to be covered by The Next Estate and an 18-hole golf course designed by Jack Nicklaus, you could call them the Nicklai Indians. There's no evidence that they golfed, though."

Litner said in a letter in June to Next Estate officials that it was probable that prehistoric Indians commonly roamed the area and that it would be 'desirable' to conduct an archaeological survey of the lands to search for Indian artifacts before any widespread construction begins at The Next Estate. Overall, Litner thinks the study of vanished Indians is more valuable than an exclusive sanctuary for amateur golfers.

"Archaeologically, we can gain more useful knowledge from examining Indian artifacts than from examining golf balls," he said. "If we wanted to study golf, we'd watch the PGA tour on TV. Prehistoric Indians, on the other hand, aren't shown on the Saturday programs."

What Janice wanted to know was how I got Litner to call them the Nicklai Indians.

"I just told him that's what *we* decided to call them," I

said. "And in the interview, he decided he might as well call them that, too."

Janice grinned and put her leg over mine, saying, "So now we've named an Indian tribe. It's got to be true. It's in the *paper.*"

"I know. Isn't it fun?"

# 35

Sometimes a newspaper story was like a handful of rocks thrown with your eyes closed. You were likely to hit someone, but you didn't know who until they screamed.

Daniel Garn screamed. Garn, a professor of archaeology at the university, was mad at Gerald Litner and me for the invention of the Nicklai tribe. Janice and I saw Garn on the TV news Monday night denouncing Litner and, he said, "the idiotic reporter for the *News-Dispatch* who wrote that irresponsible refuse."

"That's you," Janice said in a slightly alarmed tone.

Garn was mad that Litner and the idiotic reporter "shamelessly defamed and trivialized the admirable and extremely difficult lives of unknown Indians who struggled on this continent centuries before the first European profiteers set foot on North America."

"Stupid dick," I said to the TV.

"In a time when America is supposed to be working toward more social enlightenment . . ."

"Oh, kiss my ass."

". . . and an intolerance of bigotry," Garn said, "I find it embarrassing and repugnant that a supposedly respected archaeologist and a major daily paper have slandered Indians by suggesting they might be named after Jack Nicklaus."

It wasn't even news. It was dumb drama from a man who had no grasp of irony and why I'd even thought of naming the Indians the Nicklai tribe. But thousands of people saw it on TV, so now they thought it was news and that I'd demeaned the Indians I'd actually defended. Garn's moralistic blather on TV was fundamentally repeated in tedious letters mailed to the various local papers, the text of which was printed in our paper and included a demand that I apologize to all American Indians for my "senseless and odious slander of Indians."

Perrault used this occasion to write another bombastic memo from the depths of his shallow brain:

A recent public outcry accusing this paper of defaming American Indians unfortunately has some merit. Again we find lazy editing and lazy reporting in a story that named prehistoric Indians who once lived where The Next Estate is being constructed as the "Nicklai Indians," even though no such tribe ever existed and it's obviously a clever and atrocious reference to professional golfer Jack Nicklaus.

Explanations for this error are due.

Christopher called me at the bureau and said he was told by Perrault that we had to write a correction.

"It's impossible to write a correction. I didn't make a mistake," I said.

"Of course you didn't. But Perrault insists we run a correction," Christopher said.

"Doesn't he know a fucking thing?"

"He knows his name, and he knows yours. That could be dangerous for you."

"Well, I can't write a correction."

"Be imaginative, Kurt. That's what keeps getting you in trouble. Use it to your advantage. You don't have to write a genuine correction. I recommend you weasel your way out of it and think up something wry, but not too snotty, and make believe it's a correction. If all we do is put the word 'correction' at the top of it, Perrault will think it's a correction. And keep the fucker short. Perrault tires easily."

Writing a correction when an error wasn't made was hard. To concentrate, I had to go to the Bookmark Cafe

& Bookstore, sit at a little table and drink coffee and twirl my hair absentmindedly while trying to write a correction that wasn't a correction. After nine or ten experimental drafts, I decided this was close:

> Correction: An article in Sunday's edition of the *News-Dispatch* referring to the "Nicklai Indians" in Wellington County might have mistakenly led some readers to believe that Jack Nicklaus was named after prehistoric Indians. Archaeologists have no evidence that prehistoric Indians golfed. Indians did, however, invent lacrosse.

To me, it seemed confusing enough to avoid being a correction while still resembling one. I was pleased.

# 36

One ordinary morning after everyone arrived at work, we faced the eerie and metaphysical emergency that all newspapers eventually couldn't avoid. There was no news.

No one knew of or even suspected the possible existence that day of anything genuinely worth writing about that sensibly could be called news.

"You mean, *no* one has any stories?" Lisa asked, staring at us huddled together in listless apathy at the ten o'clock meeting.

"There's no news," I said, holding out my empty hand.

"Nothing," Harmon said.

"Not really," Rebecca said.

"Blank," Theresa said.

"Double blank," Marta announced.

"It ain't there," Donny said.

Lisa seemed to accept this as a tentative truth, that the circumstances of life had so poorly aligned themselves that day that something called news refused to be there. Like the rest of us, she seemed jaded and apathetic. She pulled a rubber band out of her purse and began twirling her hair into a ponytail that she held in place with the rubber band. Then we sat in a lazy stupor on this newsless day.

"What *is* news, anyway?" Rebecca said.

"News is when some shit happens and you write about it," I said.

"Very *good,* Kurt," Lisa said. "Did you learn that in journalism school?"

"Don't accuse me of going to journalism school," I said.

"I apologize," Lisa said. "Well. What can we do, now that there's no news?"

"Sleep," Donny said.

"Go home and have sex with your husband," Marta said.

"What if you don't have a husband?" Harmon asked.

"Ask some man to marry you," Rebecca said.

And we were quiet again, like the eerie, newsless day was a toxic, numbing cloud making us sleepy and useless. Lisa drank some coffee and stared pointlessly at the floor.

"This happens sometimes," she said in a tired, distant voice.

"Could we just print a note on the front page saying 'There's no news today: Fuck you'?" Harmon said sort of indifferently.

Not even looking at Harmon, Lisa said, "Probably not."

"Okay," Harmon said.

I knew what it was. Probably by coincidence alone, each of us on the same day was weary and disgusted with the fundamental idea of news as this universally important thing that everyone in the public urgently wanted to see, when, actually, most people didn't care what we wrote anyway, and almost none of it could be described correctly as very important. It was sad, kind of, to have to realize you were in a profession where you at least earnestly hoped you were writing things that people found interesting and useful, but frequently you were just filling up the white space next to the department-store ads. Few things in life were genuinely so interesting or urgent that they deserved to be told immediately, in detail, seven days a week. In a way, reporters were like little kids running around saying, "Lookit! Lookit!" about every ordinary thing no one wanted to see very much. It was painful when you realized that all at once. It resulted in a newsless day, like this one.

Harmon rubbed a finger slowly across his lips, then said in a distracted voice, "Maybe an army transport plane will crash into a kindergarten."

"Quit trying to be optimistic," I said. "You have no right to violate our apathy."

"Sorry," Harmon said.

As reporters, we were forced to treat this newsless day as if it were an ordinary day.

"I know nothing's happening. Write about it anyway," Lisa said, walking dispiritedly back to her office, followed a second or two later by Harmon with a preoccupied look on his face, as if he was thinking of something that wasn't quite there in his disordered and unkempt mind. To clear my head of extraneous thoughts and make room for some superfluous ones, I sat at my desk and used a North Carolina Division of Environmental Management press release on toxins in the public waterways to make an advanced paper airplane. It was advanced in the sense that it required intricate folding and precise symmetry, as well as some little flaps on the wings to give it superior lift useful in doing rolls and flips. What bothered me about modern architecture then was that the walls and ceiling of the bureau were too close in to allow for a really adequate flight for my airplane, unless I wanted it to constantly crash into things, which to me contravened the whole purpose of my being there that morning. Although if I remained idle and sufficiently estranged from the ability to think of news on our newsless day, I might not have to write anything at all, thus giving me time to think of something to write when it didn't matter anymore. Good.

"Kurt," Harmon called out in a slightly high-pitched, officious-sounding tone, the one he used when he discovered an idea he wanted to inflict on someone else. He was gesturing at me from the doorway of Lisa's office.

"Kurt, c'mere. We got a story for you," he said.

It didn't make sense that either of them would have gotten a story for me, just for me, when no one at *all* had any; as if something in Harmon's disordered mind had conceived a particular story that *he* didn't want to do and he went to persuade Lisa to make *me* do it.

I went into the office, where Lisa glanced at me then looked down at a university press release on her desk. Harmon was gnawing on one of his fingernails like a hamster, staring distractedly at me.

"Here's a story you'd be good at," Lisa said. "A feature on national viruses."

"You mean that movie Elizabeth Taylor was in when she was a girl?" I said.

"That's *National Velvet*," Harmon said.

"I like my title better," I said. "And what's a *national* virus? One that has a cultural and political heritage?"

Lisa shook her head no. "The University Department of Epidemiology has a press release here on all the statistical work they do, saying they got a two-million-dollar grant to help track the rise and decline of AIDS across the nation," she said.

Janice.

"No," I said.

"What do you mean no?"

"I won't do it." I'd never refused to do a story before, never bluntly told an editor I wasn't going to have anything to do with my job.

"It's a good story," Harmon said.

"Fuck you, Harmon."

"What's going on?" Lisa said worriedly, staring at Harmon and then me.

"I can't do the story because my girlfriend works for the department of epidemiology. She compiles all those statistics you want me to write about. Harmon knows that, don't you, Harmon?"

"But, Kurt, it's a good story, and you don't have to interview Janice," he said in a kind of wounded and indignant tone.

"Is Janice your girlfriend?" Lisa asked.

It seemed like Harmon thought it was funny that he'd maneuvered me into possibly having to write about Janice and treating her like news. He was trying not to smirk. I tensed my muscles.

"What if I shatter your skull?" I said to Harmon. "Could that be a feature story?"

He flinched. It looked like Lisa did, too.

"Well, Kurt, you certainly don't have to interview your girlfriend, at least not if she's going to be a major part of the story, which she shouldn't be because she's your girlfriend," Lisa said in an appeasing voice.

"I shouldn't interview her for *any* reason, and Harmon, let's walk down the street so I can throw you in front of a truck. You're heavy, but if I get a running start, I know I could throw you at least ten feet. Does death finally scare you, you stupid dick? Does *anything* matter to you? Your own blood, for example?" I walked to the edge of Harmon's shoes like I could knock him down with his own fear, wondering if I should put my hand under his chin and shove his head through the wall.

"It's just a story, Kurt," he said cautiously. "It's not personal."

"Everything's personal when it happens to you," I said, putting my hand on his shoulder in a friendly manner and squeezing down to the bone.

"Let go," Harmon said peevishly.

"I guess intimacy scares you," I said. "I'm glad something does."

# 37

The doctor in charge of the two-million-dollar grant said she scarcely had time to talk with reporters and that I'd need to call the project supervisor, who, when I reached her, was on her way to Atlanta and had no time to talk with reporters, saying I'd have to contact the chief assistant researcher on the project, Janice Galassi.

"I can't," I said.

"You can't? I don't understand," the project supervisor said curiously and impatiently.

"The chief assistant researcher, as you call her, is my girlfriend."

"Janice? So you're Janice's boyfriend."

"Yes, ma'am."

"Well, why can't you interview her, for God's sake? You're obviously quite comfortable with her already," she said.

"I'm supposed to be objective. If you interview your girlfriend, people might say you're not objective."

"I don't *have* a girlfriend," she said. "Well, I do see your problem, though."

"Also, I'd feel a little strange treating Janice as news."

"Yes. But you don't mind treating *me* as news," she said a little caustically.

"That's different," I said apologetically.

"I know. I'm not your girlfriend. But I'm sorry to tell you that it doesn't matter anyway, because I'm leaving for the airport now. You'll just have to interview Janice."

I went to Lisa's office and said, "Lisa. You're a woman."

"I've known that for years, Kurt," she said.

"So is it all right if I interview a woman I'm in love with?"

"You mean your girlfriend?"

"Yes. That's whose girlfriend I'm in love with."

"But can't you talk with someone else at the university?"

"No. Everyone's busy. They won't talk with me. They keep saying I have to interview the chief assistant researcher, who happens to be my chief primary only exclusive girlfriend, Janice," I said, sighing loudly.

"I've never faced a problem like this before," she said.

"And you still aren't. Janice isn't your girlfriend."

"Well," she said.

"Well," I said.

It was Lisa's turn to say well again.

"We have to have that story," she said tiredly.

"Make Harmon do it. That little fucker did this on purpose. I want to pull his windpipe out and blow on it."

Lisa shook her head. "I've got him on another story. In fact, even though everyone said this was a newsless day, everyone's already working on stories, so I can't just switch stories around."

"So I'm going to interview my girlfriend," I said. "Would it violate journalistic ethics if I rubbed her thigh during the interview?"

"But this isn't really a conflict-of-interest story, Kurt. It's a piece about epidemiology and statistics, right? You couldn't be doing anything in print that would obviously or even slightly be construed as doing her a favor."

"If I kissed her neck," I said.

"You could do a *phone* interview," she said.

"Oh. Phone sex. It's too remote for me."

She exhaled audibly and thumped the palm of her hand on her forehead, saying "Kurt. I'm sorry this happened, but we have to do the story. This is a slow news day and I've already promised this story on the budget."

"Fuck," I said quietly.

"No, Kurt. You have to remain objective," she said.

# 38

"**E**pidemiology. Galassi speaking," she said.

"Act like you don't know me and you're not in love with me and we've never been as one before so I can pretend to be professionally disinterested and interview you about the two-million-dollar grant, national viruses, and shit like that," I said all in one sudden sentence to get it over with quickly.

"Kurt? What in the hell are you talking about?" she said with amused confusion.

"I can't explain it, so all I'll do is explain it," I said. "Janice. Today when I didn't have a story to work on, Harmon took a press release to Lisa suggesting I do a feature story on the two-million-dollar grant you guys got to study

AIDS. No one else can do it, Lisa says we have to have it today, and your two bosses whose names I don't remember are both too busy to be interviewed, so they both said I had to talk with you. I have to interview you, unless *you* say you're too busy. Could you do that? Tell me you're not there."

"Kurt. I'm here."

"Couldn't you leave, so only the most ignorant and unhelpful people are there who couldn't possibly be interviewed?"

"They really want you to interview *me*? Don't they know I'm your girlfriend?"

"Yes, and they all want me to make believe it doesn't matter. I told Lisa I'd do a phone interview so it wouldn't seem like favoritism if I caressed your thighs."

"Are you saying this on the phone at work?"

"No. I'm at the pay phone at Stanley's."

"What're you doin' *there*, Kurt?"

"It's more private than the bureau."

"Good Lord," she said in a puzzled tone. "You mean you talked with Dr. Samner and Carol Eisen and *both* of them can't talk with you?"

"I forget their names, but one of them just said she had no time for reporters and the other one, Eisen, I think, said she was going to the airport to go to Atlanta."

"And they said to interview *me*?"

"Yes. Does this mean you're intelligent or something?"

"Or something," she said. "Well, Kurt, I'd love to talk with you."

"Janice, that's *good*, but don't *say* that. You're supposed to lie to me and say you're going to Copenhagen or something so I don't have to interview you."

"Why don't you want to interview me?"

"You remind me too much of my girlfriend."

"Are you afraid I'll say dumb things?"

"Janice. I don't *want* to call you up and treat you with professional indifference, and quiz you and query you and turn you into a piece of news, goddammit."

"Well, I'm glad, Kurt. I feel better now. Where do you want to query me?" she said in a soft voice.

"I don't."

"Oh, Kurt. I love it when you query me."

"Stop it."

She began breathing rapidly. "Do you want to do it over the phone?"

"I'm not sure."

"I'm by myself in my office, Kurt. The door's closed. No one will know I'm being queried," she said in a low, sensual voice.

"Maybe we should do it in person."

"Oh yes. Oh *yes*," she moaned. "And let's do it *on* the record."

"Couldn't we do it on the floor?"

Her breathing intensified, growing louder and quicker. "Oh, Kurt. Let's do it on a legal pad."

"Janice. Stay in your office. Keep the door closed until I get there. I'm leaving now."

# 39

Taped onto the bathroom mirror with jaggedly torn sections of masking tape was a crumpled copy of the metro section with my story in it, the interview, and this note scrawled on it in blue ink: *It's not funny to me.* My stomach began to sting and burn, like acid, and a panic went through me so quickly it seemed as if I quit breathing for two or three seconds and was suddenly sweating and slammed my head into the doorway because I couldn't see or forgot to see, realizing I'd hurt Janice, rushing through me the panic that she could be gone. I called her at work, the woman on the phone saying she was at lunch. I was supposed to eat but my stomach was burning. I went back to the bathroom, looking at the crumpled story on the mir-

ror, *it's not funny to me,* drinking some water from the faucet
which I threw up into the toilet, praying to Jesus that whatever I'd done I'd know, that it would be explained, Janice
showing her pain to me I'd try to take it back from her,
absorbing all of it although I couldn't absorb her pain even
if she'd allow me the attempt. Looking again at the paper
on the mirror, trying to make my eyes focus on the print
and whatever I'd done wrong, I read the lead saying: "A
$2 million grant for AIDS research by epidemiologists at
the University of St. Beaujolais comes out to about $2.99
per AIDS sufferer in America, or approximately the cost
of a breakfast at Shoney's."

Maybe the injury was there, contrasting an AIDS
grant with how much it was worth per person per breakfast. I didn't know and couldn't have known, having no
knowledge of whatever hurt her except that I came home
for lunch and saw the crumpled newspaper taped on the
bathroom mirror, not even thinking of returning to work
then but waiting and waiting for Janice to get back to her
office and I'd find out what I'd done and how far she'd
moved from me that morning alone. I called again and she
was in.

Cautiously I said, "Janice, what did I do? I saw the
paper in the bathroom."

"You don't even know," she said distantly.

"I don't. You have to tell me."

"That's just it. I don't *want* to tell you. You didn't know

to begin with that anything you could do so goddamn clev-
erly in the paper could have any effect on me, even though
we were lovers."

She said were. "Did the lead make you angry?" I said.

"And why would that make me angry?" she said quietly. "Why would I care that a newspaper story with *me* in
it, representing *my* department and a major grant makes
the public imagine we're all happily, joyously comparing
the deaths of thousands of people with breakfast at Sho-
ney's?"

She was both angry and hurt, and it wasn't going to
end. Nor was there anything sensible or useful I could
say then to explain why I did it or why I was stupid or
that I was sorry for her because it wouldn't reverse anything or even seem honorable. But I said, "I'm sorry, Janice."

"Well, I'm sorrier," she said. "I'm writing letters to my
bosses today explaining in detail that I said nothing at all
to make you believe the department of epidemiology com-
pares the worth of this grant to an ordinary breakfast,
Kurt, because they might *think* that's what I told you."

"But it's just *me*, the reporter, doing that. Won't they
realize that?"

"They will when they get my letters, which they can
use to explain to anyone else who asks, after reading your
story today, if everyone at work is just having a lot of
damn fun trivializing AIDS. And they *will* think that,

Kurt; just because you introduced the idea. And it doesn't matter that it's a harmless, clever idea. People are going to wonder if we've diminished the awful seriousness of this disease because it was so important to you to write something that pleased you. Well, it didn't please *me,* Kurt. You didn't even *tell* me you were doing that. You didn't call me and say, 'Hey, guess what I've decided to write, Janice. I've decided to make your job seem fun and amusing, and screw the world if they don't like it.' And damn you for it, too, Kurt. It really hurt me, just goddamn hurt me to pick up the paper and read what you did, with no thought at all how it might affect me at work. So think about it now. I want you to stay away from the apartment for a while and don't call me. You hurt me, Kurt, and you didn't even know. Well, *know* it for a while."

And she hung up.

I didn't. I dumbly held the phone to my ear as if she might be there again, even when the phone just buzzed. Before I cried, which I knew was going to happen in its pathetic and pointless way, I thought of praying again, praying that Janice would stop being hurt, that my sentence in the paper would be regarded as harmless by everyone, that Janice wouldn't leave me, and that I'd learn to know what might hurt Janice so I wouldn't do it; and even after I did it, prayed that prayer, I knew it wasn't going to work, that pain always grew and gathered strength in its ordinary duty to smother us, and today I was its creator. It didn't come from some random force in the world. It came from me.

And then I didn't cry, possibly because I deserved pain, but not the luxury of my own sadness.

# 40

The psychiatrist said you aren't cured. You never are. The people who think they're cured are the most lethal because, having satisfactorily and wondrously pronounced themselves healed because it's so awful not to be, they naturally enjoy the delusion of being normal and ordinary and so they have one harmless beer or one harmless glass of wine or an obviously innocent mixed drink. Just one, as a public, celebratory ritual to prove that they aren't alcoholics because they don't *deserve* being alcoholics. Belief supplants fact. I'm well, I'm well. Don't worry, be happy. Reality only exists when I invent it, and so on. But when you take that drink and recognize its taste and feel that peculiar warm rush resulting in elation or euphoria, it's no longer a celebration of being cured but a resumption of your slow and ugly suicide. You might as well jump into a blast furnace. It's quicker.

We don't have any blast furnaces around here. Will I have to drive to Pittsburgh for that? That's too far.

She said there will be stresses and fears and sadnesses you can't avoid, and you'll want to drink quite badly, like in the wine commercials on TV, with pretty, well-dressed women your age who appear to be so bright and healthy and voluptuous and sane as they chit-chat happily and have their friendly intimacies, and *they* aren't dying, *they* aren't being crushed with anxiety and depression as they cheerfully drink their delicate wine. But you are. What will you do when there's a great loss in your life?

Hurt.

Yes, you will. And you'll be tempted to drink, because it's the most exquisite painkiller and sedative you know. Do you use any other drugs?

Love.

Love's not a drug, generally.

It could be. The Food and Drug Administration wouldn't be able to regulate it.

Actually, love can be addictive.

I don't know why I talk to you. You depress me. Do you need a doctoral degree to depress me, or can less qualified people do it?

. . .

At home, which wasn't really home but just this building I was in filled with the constant absence of Janice, a complex emotional need that, once constructed, now had no source, a beer commercial came on TV with people dancing in the desert and a woman in her long summer dress smiling with love and sex and the personal moisture you could only smell up close, along with Michelob Dry. Everything was a complete, stunning absence, a hollowness in me that was expanding and getting hollower, as if I was overcome by the intense presence of nothing. My head felt swollen and I was afraid and put all the weights I had on my long steel bar, not even adding up the weights to wonder how heavy it was, just symmetrically arranging all of the weights on opposite ends and lifting it all over my head in such pain and wobbling violence to imagine, without hope, that I might exhaust myself enough to sleep, or exterminate my consciousness.

Which failed, and I knew I could go to the store, although Janice would be hurt by this, and buy dry sherry to numb my head and give me a kind of warm tranquillity that couldn't be shared or even healed. It didn't seem like Dante put any alcoholics in hell. Maybe this was wise. People who had tranquillity that needed to be healed would have found hell a little bit primitive.

To prevent or at least delay what was looking like the renewed slaughter of myself through incurable tranquillity, I went to an AA meeting. The only requirement you had to meet to attend an AA meeting was that something was wrong with you. I was qualified. When I walked into the room, trying not to seem anxious or not to seem peculiarly calm or not to seem like I was seeming anything, I thought about walking up to one of the people, introducing myself, and saying the only thing I didn't like about AA meetings was that they let so many alcoholics in.

A few of the people I recognized from the last meeting I'd been to about five months ago, although most of them were strangers to me and probably strangers to each other. Of the thirty or forty people scattered across the room in plastic chairs or going into the little kitchen to fill styrofoam cups with hot coffee to have with their cigarettes, the majority were men, as if men were more reliable alcoholics than women. There were maybe a dozen women, and when I studied them casually and wondered what had happened to them, they looked as if they'd been hurt at least as well as the men. I didn't think anybody should hurt that well, but the room was filled with them. Us.

I wondered where Janice was, if she was having dinner at home or if she went out, maybe to talk with a more sane and pleasant man than me who would smile at her and not be a sudden and bewildering injury to her like I was, which was going to make me cry but I was trying to believe that being sad wasn't a privilege of mine anymore. I was the only one who knew about *this* drama, pretending I couldn't hurt because Janice did. Being crazy and fractured was for me just too convenient. I wanted Janice to see me there and love me, to walk in the room and pull me out. That was just magic, and I never had magic.

The room was loud with private chatter and mumbling and some laughter before the meeting began, with people split up like at a party in their personal groups, or with solitary people sitting in pure quiet in all this noise, holding themselves in or holding themselves down, some of them looking as wounded and frantic as I was the night I quit drinking and had nothing to occupy me but endless panic. Nothing would actually characterize the whole group or be its identifying description. There was always too much detail, most of it hidden and never spoken, but in the two times I'd been to meetings before and this time, I always thought of the people as pretty brave to gather there with their common disease, one that was still despised and maligned as if they had knowingly and premeditatedly become ill, satisfying the public's desire for a contemptible enemy. I thought they were pretty brave just to look at each other. And me. I was one of them, too, although I had a neat psychological tendency, and I assumed others did also, to imagine myself to be among the best of the alcoholics, whatever that meant; as if in our fraternity of controlled illness, *my* disease wasn't quite as severe as other people's, or I was blessed with an ability to endure my disease more admirably and with less effort, like I'd get a fucking prize for the complexity and grace of my pain. Pain could be funny, if you did it right.

I didn't even know why I was there, unless it was the unbearable absence of Janice. And suddenly a concealed part of me, the demon who is just me, assumes it's now time to resume drinking because it gives you peace when no one else does. And even when you defeat that, it always comes back, waiting to placidly seduce you, which isn't hard. There is the sense that even when you are okay, you really aren't.

The man, some leader of the group, called for everyone's attention and established the beginning of the meeting, which was no more than everyone being quiet now, as anyone at all talked for a while about what was hurting them and scaring them, or some successes they were having. The ritual was to say your first name only and say you were an alcoholic, then begin talking about anything you wanted, which could get awfully sad, such as when a young woman named Dolores explained to us that she was already manic-depressive and one week ago she drank a quart of Tequila and began vomiting blood. It was like listening to ghosts, listening to characters from Dante's *Inferno* who'd been temporarily excused from hell to come to this room and describe what they hoped to escape, if something would only work. And we didn't know what was supposed to work, except the religion of not doing. I wouldn't really call it a church, since you couldn't look in a phone book and find the First Church of Not Doing, or Our Lady of Not Doing. But that was our religion, in a primitive and desperate sense. The veterans there, the guardians of the

AA doctrine, probably would've said Not Doing certainly wasn't a religion because actually they wanted you to have faith in Christ, insisting that this faith was the single power that could defeat alcoholism, but even so, that still made Not Doing a religion. The Church of Last Resort. It was odd to me that Christianity was this haven for alcoholics when you considered that during communion in Christian churches, you drank wine. I wondered if you could kneel at the altar one Sunday and, as the priest bent over to you with the wine in the chalice, say, "Don't tell me Christ's blood has *alcohol* in it."

Something that began to annoy me was the ritual in which each speaker said only their first name and always added "and I'm an alcoholic." The whole point of us being there was that *all* of us were alcoholics, and I found it kind of dumbly dramatic to make everyone say "and I'm an alcoholic." Maybe this was good for some of us, to publicly acknowledge being an alcoholic, as if saying so in front of several dozen people cleansed them or helped make them brave. But it still annoyed me. It made me want to act as if it were my turn to speak, and I'd stand up, glance around the room to acknowledge the presence of everyone there, then say, "My name's Kurt, and I'm a Sagittarian."

Janice would have liked that, unless I was never going to see her again.

# 41

Janice was holding her gun when I walked into her apartment carrying a tree. It was the eighth day of our estrangement and an attempt at our reunion, a moment made particularly odd when I noticed, as Janice closed the door and smiled at me in a kind of tentative way, that she had the Beretta in her hand, dangling it loosely toward the floor. Holding the little potted tree in front of my chest with both hands, I said, "Hi."

"Hi," she said in a cheerful but subdued way, as if we both were hiding our emotions, planning on bringing them out one by one, but guarding them now.

"You have a gun," I said.

"You have a tree," she replied, smiling at the Norfolk

pine and then at me, where my face was visible behind the tree.

"Are you going to shoot me?"

Her smile became a little more serious now, and she shook her head from side to side. "No," she said dreamily, as if remembering something far away. I wondered if it was me, right there but so distant I was gone. "I invited you here for dinner and to talk. I think it would be impolite to shoot you."

"Why are you holding the gun?"

"Oh," she said, lightly laughing at herself. "I guess it does look threatening. I'm sort of absentminded for some reason. Before you got here and I was straightening up, I put some papers in the desk drawer and saw the gun. I took it out because my father said I need to clean it sometime. And then you were here. What are you doing with that tree?"

"It's for you. I thought of getting you some flowers but *all* men bring flowers to women, and I never do what all men do. So I got you a tree. It's a Norfolk pine. I'll give you this tree if you put the gun away. Or, you could just rob me."

"How much money do you have?"

"About twenty-five dollars."

"That's not enough for a good robbery," she said, walking to the desk to put the gun away. "Do I still get the tree?"

"Yes. Do you like Norfolk pines?"

"They're beautiful. And why do you want me to have a tree?" she said as she took the tree from my hands and carried it to the end of the couch, placing it on the floor there.

"I want to be nice to you. I want to stop hurting you, and I want to be forgiven, if that's possible, and I realize it might not be. I want this maddening pain to end for both of us and to be your lover and your friend again, or at least your friend, if nothing else is possible. So I got you a tree. Even if you don't keep me, you get to keep the tree."

She was turned sideways in the room, staring down at the tree and holding her fingers to her cheeks as if thinking again of something that wasn't there. Something was gone. Me, it seemed.

"What do you mean it might not be possible to be forgiven?" she said in a puzzled and somewhat irritated voice, still staring at the tree. "Are you realizing my choices for me, in case I won't do that? I get to think up all my choices."

"I didn't mean . . ."

"Don't tell me what you didn't mean. Tell me what you *did* mean. If I don't keep you, I still get the tree?" she said curiously, not looking at me yet.

"It was a joke."

"Your choices are so limited. You, or a tree. Maybe I'll just keep the tree. All I have to do is water it and give it light. Maintaining you is a lot harder," she said, walking into the kitchen to look at something in a pan on the stove. "I have my tree. You can go, now."

Without knowing how, we'd confused and deepened our pain. What was supposed to have been our reunion dinner resulted in my being replaced by a tree. This silliness was starting to hurt too much. I thought that whatever I'd say next would be wrong, and whatever I didn't say would also be wrong. Janice poured herself a glass of red wine and took a big drink, which I knew was meant to relax her. I didn't get to relax.

"I'd give you some wine, but you don't drink," she said in a quiet and calm voice, still not looking at me as she held a wooden spoon and slowly stirred the sauce or something in the pan. "How are you doing?"

"Fine."

"No. You're not. We're having a fight."

"I know. I wish we'd have something else. I went to an AA meeting a few nights ago."

"You did?"

"I was afraid I might go buy some beer, or I was at least thinking of it, not very seriously, so I went to the AA meeting."

"How was it?"

"It was pretty casual. They let a bunch of alcoholics in."

She looked over at me curiously. It seemed like she was going to smile but decided against it, then resumed not looking at me and stirring whatever was in the pan. I kept standing in front of the coffee table, right where I'd been when I handed her the tree, as if nothing was safe or known or proper enough for me to move, like I might have to leave suddenly because I didn't belong there anymore, or because we were so hurt, it wouldn't be right to sit down and be comfortable, but it wouldn't be right to walk into the kitchen and be near her, because it was being decided if we could have each other. She opened a cabinet and got a glass out. I watched her the way you might watch a priest or a doctor at work, as if every movement was a crucial and precise act leading to a new future controlled by them. She opened the freezer and put ice into the glass. She opened the refrigerator and took out a big bottle of Coke, then unscrewed the cap and filled the glass with Coke.

"Come get your Coke," she said, holding the glass out to me and making me walk into the kitchen to be near her. I wouldn't look at her eyes, as if that were too private, an intimate privilege I'd lost. I took the glass from her hand, being careful not to touch her fingers. She put her other hand on my chest, just lightly resting the palm of her hand and her fingers on my chest. I was glad, but didn't know if I should say so. Everything I did was a potential error, one more being enough to hurt her again and make her decide to get rid of me. The way we were now, I was already gone. We were in the same room together, but missing. She patted my chest and turned around to study things on the stove. It was tomato sauce.

"I'll tell you what hurt me," she said, and sipped some

red wine. "You didn't even think, when you wrote your story, that my job mattered or that you could have an effect on me. You did what you often do at work, which was to take an entire story and its relevant facts, which you got correctly, and reduce them to a form of amusement for yourself. I know that's your style, and sometimes you do it brilliantly, but sometimes things are more *important* than that and don't deserve to be just one more witty, sardonic amusement for yourself. And especially *me*, Kurt," she said, stopping to scrape some tomato sauce from the sides of the pan with the wooden spoon. "You weren't writing about some abstract, remote meeting, or a government policy or some high-altitude bureaucrats you'd never even see so it didn't *matter* what you said about them or how you subtly or blatantly constructed a description to have fun. You were writing about *me*, Kurt. My job. My career. My concerns, and *my* goddamn emotions. But you couldn't tell it when the story came out. When I picked that paper up and read the first line, it was like I was being attacked and ridiculed by you," she said, stirring the tomato sauce a little more violently.

"Of course you weren't de*libe*rately attacking me, but it was almost worse than that because you'd obviously written something funny and potentially damaging without even guessing I could feel this way. You de*meaned*," she said, creating little waves of red sauce in the pan, "my work, my responsibilities and me. And to you, it was an innocent amusement. AIDS research compared to breakfast at Sho-ney's?" she said contemptuously, whacking the spoon on the edge of the pan to dislodge a gob of tomato sauce. "When did a fatal epidemic become funny, Kurt? And why was my job just a goddamn occasion for you to be clever?"

There was nothing to defend. I was guilty. My impulse was to be punished as long as she felt I deserved it. She looked back angrily at me, as if my silence was a new of-fense.

"Aren't you going to talk?" she said.

"No. I can't defend myself because you're right. I stu-pidly hurt you without realizing it could happen. Your crit-icisms are completely correct and fair. I was a self-willed, witless son of a bitch."

"Yes, you were," she said, and began stirring the sauce even though it was already stirred and almost frothy. "And what should I do now? Forgive you because that would be nice? I don't feel like being nice. I feel hurt and cheated, like you didn't take me any more seriously than just a for-tunate excuse for being funny. I exist too, goddamn you. All of my emotions and impulses are there just as strongly as yours, and I'm *not* some piece of material to be toyed with in a goddamn story. I don't think I want a lover who has to be reminded that I'm real."

This scared me.

"Are you leaving me?" I said quietly.

She stopped stirring the tomato sauce and sighed.

"I'm not leaving you. I'm fixing *dinner.* If I were leaving you, I wouldn't feed you, you idiot. Do you think I'm such a nice woman that I'd give you an I'm-Leaving-You dinner? Good God. And quit standing behind me so quietly like a prisoner about to be killed. If I wanted to kill you, I would've shot you at the door. At least tell me you're sorry."

I walked behind her and leaned my face against her head. "I'm sorry."

Reaching behind her, she put her arm around my neck as if to hug me, then increased the pressure enough to begin lightly choking me against her shoulder.

"You really hurt me," she said quietly as she choked me.

"I didn't mean to. I can't be forgiven if you choke me to death."

"I'm not squeezing that hard yet," she said, holding me to her affectionately enough to make unconsciousness seem imminent.

# 42

Christopher met me at the Same Place bar in Hampton to warn me that the qualities that made me valuable were also the ones that would make me fail. But first he decided to ridicule me for not drinking bourbon, like him, because I ordered a cup of coffee from the bartender.

"I'm embarrassed to be seen with you. It's un-American to drink coffee in a bar," he said, playfully chiding me, without having any idea that I'd lived in a disabling panic for two days when I quit drinking.

"I'm not an American. I was born in Texas," I said.

He sighed and scowled at me and my coffee, saying, "What are you, a born-again, charismatic, viper-fondling Christian?"

"I don't join clubs."

He nodded his head approvingly, then lit a Pall Mall from the butt of the Pall Mall he hadn't finished smoking. Swallowing his double bourbon in two gulps, he ordered another one by holding up his index finger toward the bartender. Once he had his new drink and took a sizable sip, reminding me of the pleasure of alcohol rapidly poisoning your brain so that whatever hurt you seemed absent, when, really, it was just some of your consciousness going away, I said, "So is this a meeting or what?"

"Sort of," he said. "I just called you here to warn you about yourself. You're doing a good enough job as a reporter it could fling you entirely out of this profession."

"What's that mean?"

"It means a lot. I think when I hired you, I remember saying something like there's something wrong with you. It might be valuable."

"Yes, and why are you warning me about myself?"

"Well, it's not something you don't already know about, Kurt. Practically everything that makes you valuable as a reporter is precisely what most editors loathe, particularly Perrault. Most newspaper editors think of the readers as dull mammals with a single impulse to acquire facts, and a fact is any knowledge generally robbed of its complexity and undecorated with any emotion or irony or humanness. A true journalist, which you're incapable of being, always tries to write a story as if simple factuality is all that matters. You're not a true journalist. I don't know *what* you are."

"A vertebrate."

Christopher sniffed his bourbon audibly, like a dog or a cat exploring for food, then took a big sip and stared off at three young women together at a table.

"Perrault despises you," he said.

"Despises? He doesn't know me well enough for that much emotion," I said.

"He doesn't need to know you at all, and wishes you were gone," Christopher said in his normal voice, without urgency or much emotion.

"Why does it matter that he despises me?"

"Yesterday when he was pissed off at virtually every story you've done in the last two months, like the Nicklai Indian episode, he called me into his office and asked why I hired you."

"What'd you tell him?"

He took another big sip of bourbon. "I told him you had substantial reporting experience, nothing excellent, but sound experience. And I told him you were a genuine writer, someone who knows why we even bother to put a single sentence on a page."

I nodded my head. "The reason we put a single sentence on a page is because most readers think *two* sentences is too much to read."

"And Perrault said he thinks you're a self-willed, arrogant butthead," Christopher said.

We were both quiet, wondering about that description.

"What do I do that he hates the most?" I said.

"Work on his paper," Christopher said.

"And why should I care? Can he comfortably despise
me for months and months, growing accustomed to my in-
tolerable existence?"

"No. He won't change, and you won't change. Or will
you? To please Perrault, all you have to do is make every
story as mundane as possible, showing no trace of yourself
and a subservient adherence to that popular distortion of
reality known as traditional journalism."

"Did he tell you that? Did he say what he wanted me
to do?"

"I don't recall precisely what he said, but he described
it as a strange experiment for me to have hired you. And
he said he was getting fucking tired of reading what he
described as your inexcusable offenses against objective
newswriting."

"Tell him not to read it. Tell him to stop reading the
paper. No one wants him to. How old is Perrault?"

"I don't know. He's in his early sixties. But that won't
help you. He's not going to die in his sleep."

"I don't want him to die. I'd like it if he passed out for
the rest of his life."

"You're a humanitarian."

"No, I'm not. I'm a Sagittarian."

"Oh. Another *s* word."

"What am I supposed to do? I mean, does he have an ultimatum or something, or did he just say he'd keep hating what I do, or what?"

"He didn't say and I didn't ask him. I think he believes that after I've told you all this, you'll get nervous and timid and become an ordinary reporter."

"What will he do the next time he reads one of my stories and can't stand it?"

Christopher drank some bourbon and lit another Pall Mall with the butt of his last one. "I really don't know. One thing he can do is ask me to fire you. But I won't do it. I told Perrault that some of your sins against journalism were worth being committed. All that did was make him angrier, as if he were being betrayed by me. He said he wanted to see some marked improvement in your work."

"Tell him it's already there."

"I don't think he's capable of knowing that. Perrault doesn't *like* talent. When he sees it, he regards it as a blight that needs to be removed."

"Is he going to remove me?"

"He could. And that's why I'm warning you. You've met a man who's fundamentally opposed to everything you do well. If you persist in writing in your style, he might fire you. If you choose to become conscientiously mundane, he might give you a raise. What I think I'm telling you, Kurt, is you have to make this decision: sink or sink."

# 43

And now I was beginning to realize there was a time when you saw failure rushing unalterably toward you and, rather than dodge it, which couldn't happen, you had to direct that failure, select it and shape it, and at least have the honor to choose and refine the course of your own ruination. So I would. It would have been too easy to go on as usual and allow Perrault's unremarkable loathing of me to result in my being fired again. That would have given Perrault the reason to get rid of me, when *I* wanted the reason to get rid of me. I think I decided that since my actions were going to ruin me anyway, I might as well ruin myself, instead of letting someone else do it. In other words, I decided to repress all my natural impulses, write exactly the way Perrault wanted me to write, and thus defeat myself before Perrault defeated me. It would be like standing in front of a firing squad and, right before they shot you, you pulled out your own gun, said, "I refuse to be shot by bastards like you," then shot yourself.

I resolved all of this secretly, to ruin myself rather than let Perrault ruin me, and I didn't tell anyone, not even Janice, but simply began this private campaign the next morning at work. Whatever I would normally doctor up or refine in my personal style I'd ignore and treat as just raw fact, raw information. What I was presented with that morning—by Lisa, so no one could say I had any bias in either selecting or rejecting it as a story—was a new lawsuit in which a woman from Cokesboro was suing the Coca-Cola Company after she found a bug like a centipede in a bottle of Coke. I mean a bug *like* a centipede, and not precisely a centipede, because neither the woman nor her lawyer could irrefutably identify the dead bug as a centipede. When I interviewed the woman, Donna Reidel, over the phone, I said, "How many legs does it have?"

"Well, I'm certainly not going to count them," she said with irritation and distaste.

"I think a centipede's supposed to have a hundred legs."

"I don't have to count them. All that matters is I found a dead bug in my Coke."

"What if it's a millipede?"

"What's that?" she wondered.

"I think it's supposed to have a *thousand* legs. Did you and your lawyer count your bug's legs, or are you just estimating?"

"I have no idea," she said.

"Well, I think a judge and also the public is going to be at least a little bit curious about whether it was a hundred legs or a thousand legs in your Coke," I said. "And, as a reporter, I'm obligated to be precise."

I wasn't going to put down in my story how the woman hung up on me. But it was exactly the innate oddness and silliness of the story that prompted Lisa to give it to me, although I refused to treat it oddly or with any respect for the dear art of silliness like I usually would. And with some sadness I wouldn't explain and didn't really understand, either, I told Lisa this was the end of my reign of silliness and personal style at the paper, and that regardless of how appropriate humor or irony might be to the dead-bug-in-the-Coke story, I no longer was going to supply it. My instinct, my most natural impulse, was to begin doing the story this way, sort of:

Donna Reidel doesn't know if the dead bug she says she found in a bottle of Coke was a centipede or a millipede.

"I don't care whose pede it was. It was in my Coke and I'm suing," she said Monday.

Or another lead I thought of after I talked briefly with a lawyer for the Coca-Cola Company in Atlanta was this:

The ingredients in Coke aren't supposed to include centipedes.

In a way it was endless, the ways you could play with the facts and still be factual. But I wasn't doing that anymore. The lead I wrote and which was printed in the paper was this one:

A Cokesboro woman filed a suit in Vermilion County against the Coca-Cola Company after allegedly finding a dead insect in a bottle of Coke.

When I wrote that lead on my computer, Lisa and I stared at it quietly, like spectators at a sorrowful accident who are nonetheless fascinated by the damage.

"Why are you writing that?" Lisa asked quietly. "It's sterile and dead."

"That's my new style," I said. "I'm giving the editors what they want. Corpses."

Everyone knew, when the morning paper came out, that something was wrong, that an unexplained decision had been made and something was ended. They looked at me, Harmon and Rebecca and the others in the bureau, the way people sort of secretively stared at someone who just got a new disease that probably was going to kill them. And it *was* going to kill me, but at my own pace and for my own reasons. All that was good about it, if self-destruction can be regarded as good, was that I controlled my own vanishment. I wondered if vanishment was a word. I liked the way it sounded. It sounded better and more noble than controlling my own destruction or doom. I at least had my vanishment to look forward to.

As I advanced nobly toward my vanishment, without even knowing exactly when I'd reach it or how I'd know when I got there, the next story I deliberately screwed up and wrote with as much lethal dullness and fatal factualism as possible came in the morning when we got a press release announcing a PLO dance in St. Beaujolais. The press release was mailed to us by a group called the American Arab League, ostensibly some national group with members at the university, and the release was essentially a flier explaining almost nothing and saying this:

PLO Dance
Live Music. Rock, Blues
& traditional Arabic
music.

Benefit concert for Palestinian families displaced in Israel and the occupied territories.

Dance sponsored by the American Arab League. $3 cover. Profits to be disbursed by the Palestine Liberation Organization.

I didn't know the PLO could dance. Ever since I'd known of them, they'd been more associated with bullets and explosions than with dancing; although it *was* true, as someone pointed out to me one day, that Yasser Arafat looked a hell of a lot like Ringo Starr. But Arafat didn't play an instrument, unless you regarded a grenade launcher as musical. Maybe you could regard it as a percussion instrument. And at least these were the natural thoughts I was having as I studied the strange task of writing a serious news story about a PLO dance at the university. It was too bizarre, the entire notion of a PLO dance. It was like announcing a fascist covered-dish supper. Or a Nazi bake sale. Or a Stalinist bingo game. Even if you intelligently and correctly realized that the Palestinian people had been violated and did deserve some kind of a national homeland, and even if you intelligently and correctly realized that at least some of the goals of the PLO were good, it was still, when you associated the PLO with dancing, just pretty damn strange. Maybe next time there'd be a PLO Easter-egg hunt. Before I called the organizers to interview them about the dance, I thought of asking them if you should bring your own sandbags and automatic weapons for the dance.

When I thought of all those Palestinian boys and teenagers throwing rocks at Israeli soldiers and police, when I imagined all those Palestinians getting years of earnest experience in skillfully throwing rocks, I wondered if they might start becoming major league pitchers. Could there be a PLO expansion team? You could call them the Occupied West Bank Dodgers. Or you could call them the Gaza White Sock, because they could only afford one sock.

Thinking of PLO baseball reminded me of Christopher Columbus. This was because in 1492, Columbus discovered the Dominican Republic, where dozens of major league baseball players are born. In fact, when Columbus was named Admiral of the Ocean Sea and set off to find a new route to reach Asia, he was the world's first baseball scout, sort of, since what he discovered was Cuba, Haiti, the Dominican Republic, Jamaica, and Puerto Rico, where about one-third of all the Earth's serious ball players were to be conceived and bred one day. I got out my baseball cards at home for some research on my PLO dance/baseball story and realized this:

Niña rhymes with Peña.

That is, Columbus's ship, the Niña, rhymes with Tony Peña, a catcher for the St. Louis Cardinals, and it rhymes with Alejandro Peña, a pitcher for the Los Angeles Dodgers. And guess what? Tony Peña was born in Montecristi, Dominican Republic. And Alejandro Peña was born in Cambiaso, Dominican Republic. What I did then, just as a cursory yet sensible check for my PLO baseball story, was use my baseball cards as a research library to compile a sample list of major-league ball players from the Caribbean. I found out that José Canseco of the Oakland Athletics was born in Havana. And so was Rafael Palmeiro, the first baseman for the Texas Rangers. And Ivan Calderon, of the Chicago White Sox, was born in Fajaro, Puerto Rico. All this made me think that when Columbus walked onshore in the Dominican Republic, he said, "I'm sent by the king and queen of Spain. We're looking for shortstops and centerfielders."

I read in a literary reference book of mine that in 1498, Columbus sailed along the coast of Venezuela. Maybe that's where he found Luis Salazar, a third baseman for the Detroit Tigers. Salazar was born in Barcelona, Venezuela. Based on this research alone, it became astonishingly clear that—

No, it didn't, really. But I was acting like it became astonishingly clear that Christopher Columbus was the father of major-league baseball. However, as my mind regressed to the subject of the PLO dance and the strange possibility of PLO baseball, I wondered if there were any Palestinians in major-league baseball. I looked through my cards and didn't find any Arabs or Palestinians, but I found Denny Martinez, a pitcher for the Montreal Expos who was born in Grenada, Nicaragua. The baseball card didn't say if he was a Contra or a Sandinista. I think he was just a pitcher.

These were my thoughts and impulses and sensibilities and natural ramblings, none of which I used when it was time for the serious reporting about the PLO dance. All I wrote in the lead was:

A dance to raise money for displaced Palestinian families in Israel will be held at the university this weekend.

Harmon looked at that lead on my computer and made a realistic puking sound.

"What's wrong with you?" he said.

"I'm fine," I said.

"That lead sucks, just like yesterday. You're not normal anymore. What's wrong with you?"

"I've decided to become normal. That's what's wrong with me."

Then came the incident of the unidentified flying omelet. Several people from the public at large and also a state trooper reported seeing something like a spaceship or a meteor or, at least, some damn thing flying in the air one night. The difficulty with such things is that because no one sees them very clearly or for very long and they don't know what happens with them when they vanish from sight, then this is what people can tell you with real certainty: hardly anything. When this trooper, Trooper Saundra Gamel, described to me over the phone how she'd seen a bluish, reddish, somewhat orange object shooting rapidly across the night sky, I asked her what she thought it was.

"An unidentified flying omelet," she said.

"What?" I said, because I couldn't quite be sure she said "omelet."

"I get so tired of people saying UFO this and UFO that when they think they mean spaceship and really they don't know at all what they've seen, so it's kind of a personal joke of mine to say that UFO stands for unidentified flying omelet," she said.

"You mean it wasn't a meteor, it was an *ome*let?"

"Might as well have been, if you don't know what it was," she said pleasantly.

"Maybe I should call up the Air Force and ask if they detected any breakfast food on their radar tonight," I said, writing that down in my notes.

"You might try it. I'm not so sure omelets show up on radar, though."

"I wonder if hash browns show up on radar."

"There's a lot we don't know."

As much as I wanted to do a factual, correct, and playful news story including the idea of unidentified flying omelets, I remained loyal to my new and lifeless prose style, and the lead I wrote was just factual: "Colored lights spotted racing through the night sky near St. Beaujolais Thursday have authorities and the public wondering."

# 44

Every day for two weeks I wrote this way, ignoring all of my natural impulses and sort of castrating or suffocating myself spiritually. I didn't know what it was supposed to lead to. My death, maybe? I didn't know what happened when you mutilated yourself emotionally for so long. But it was successful. After two weeks of this horrible self-mutilation, I was now regarded as such a promising reporter that Perrault praised me in a memo and gave me a one-hundred-dollar-a-month raise. I reacted to this honor by quitting.

It was, I decided later on in a somewhat peaceful and sullen mood, something I wanted to be able to put on my resumé; that I quit my last job because they gave me a raise.

This seemed funny, but actually being ruined hurt too much to really be very funny, and now I had no future or safety, which probably I never had anyway. I told Lisa goodbye and everyone else in the bureau goodbye, wondering how stupidly dramatic it was to quit abruptly like that, although I found the drama fully enjoyable in a kind of touching, masochistic way. Instead of letting Perrault ruin me, I ruined myself. Wasn't that better?

One didn't know. So one just walked across and down the street that evening to Stanley's for a newer and equally inexplicable drama. At the bar, where I no longer drank, I ordered a bottle of champagne.

"You don't drink, though," Nicole the bartender told me. "Remember?" she said with a cautious smile.

"You don't have to drink to order champagne," I said. "I'm celebrating my job."

"What about your job?" Nicole asked as two people I didn't know at the bar stared at me and Nicole and my bottle of champagne.

"My editor just gave me a raise, so I quit," I said, then poured a glass of champagne and pushed the glass along the bar toward this woman I didn't know, saying to her: "Here. I want you to celebrate the job I just quit. I don't drink, so you'll have to do it for me, please."

She said okay, and so did her boyfriend or whoever the man was who was with her, and without any genuine understanding of what was happening to me or how I felt,

I celebrated the loss of my job. Chief Donner came in later for dinner and walked up to me, smiling at me and the bottle of champagne in front of me.

"Are you getting married? Did you have a child?" he asked.

"I can't have children. I don't have a uterus," I said. "But here. Let me get you a glass of champagne." And I poured him some.

"And what are we celebrating?" Donner said cheerfully and uncertainly.

"My editor," I said, staring at Donner ironically or something, "the one who can't stand my existence, just gave me a one-hundred-dollar-a-month raise for agreeing to never write like myself again. So I quit."

"You quit?"

I nodded my head yes. "Either he was going to defeat me, or I was. I wanted to do it myself."

Donner looked at me with a sort of amused but serious expression, as if there was some pain I refused to mention. "He wouldn't compromise?"

"Well, I think this *is* a compromise. I'm gone," I said, sipping the coffee and whipped cream Nicole gave me as a substitute for champagne. Donner patted my back lightly and sat in the chair next to mine.

"I think you're in danger of becoming a professional outsider," he said.

"Is that a job? I need one," I said.

"No. You don't get paid for being a professional outsider. It's more of a situation."

"Like yours?"

"What? You mean the gay police chief?" he said, smiling.

"That definitely makes you a serious outsider."

"True. And that's exactly what you're getting into, I suspect."

"No. I'll never be a gay police chief. It's just not one of my ambitions."

"Well, the market around here can't hold too many, anyway, and I don't want you competing with me. But I mean I think you've made some decisions over a long period of time, even if you're not aware of them, that helped deliberately push you into the role of the professional outsider, because you sure as hell aren't an *in*-sider. You don't even have a *job*," Donner said lightly and sipped some champagne. "Do you *mind* if I talk this seriously about your private life that I know almost nothing about?"

"No. It's fine. I don't have anything left *but* a private life."

"Well, why are you doing this? I've never known anyone, except maybe me, who suddenly quit their job and endangered themselves financially for purely personal and moral reasons."

"Danger's one of the few things I'm good at."

"I believe you."

"When did *you* quit a job for purely personal, reckless reasons like me?" I asked.

"In this little city in Idaho called Soda Springs, when I was a captain on the police force. The police chief there learned that I was gay, and, unwilling to have any queer officers in the department, he ordered me to lead a raid on a supposedly gay bar in town, even though there wasn't anything illegal about gays going to a bar. And I resigned."

"That was stupid. Then you didn't have a job," I said.

"Like you? Yeah, one of the side effects of quitting is you don't have work. At least you have your honor."

"Which is worth more: honor, or money?" I said.

"Honor. 'He who steals my purse steals trash,' you know."

"Good. When I run out of money and someone comes to repossess my car, I'll kick the son of a bitch in the head and say, 'I don't need money. I have honor. Now get the fuck away from my car.' And then I'll be arrested for assault, and when they put me in jail and tell me I can post bond, I'll offer them my honor, instead of cash. And for free, they'll let me stay in jail."

"Well then, why did you quit your job, if you think money's so important?"

"Because I'm a fucking idiot. Does that sound plausible?"

"No. It's because you really have honor, and it was your choice to keep it. There are people in the world who still admire that."

"I wonder if I know them," I said.

Donner patted my back again. "You'll be okay."

"Doctors say that every day to people who die," I said.

"Well, you have to say *some*thing," Donner insisted.

This was true. Even if I wasn't going to be okay and I was going to hurt very badly for a long time, you had to say *some*thing. Which was all I was doing at the paper when I had to be punished for it. All I did was look at part of the world and describe what I saw. And when I varied too much from the orthodox descriptions of all things, when I became too distinctly myself and no longer resembled a safe, tolerable drone; no, not a drone. A news aphid, spitting up a harmless, bland batch of news goo every day; when I quit being the happy little news aphid and described how I saw the world and not how I was *told* to see it, this individualism was regarded as pathological, and I was expelled. They spit me out. Actually, the neat trick this time around was that I spit myself out. It would've been funny if it wasn't so depressing; to have destroyed myself so no one else could do it. It was getting harder and harder to call self-destruction a victory. But you had to call it *some*thing.

Before more and more of the depression leaked into me and emptied me of all hope, the one impulse I had left was to call Janice.

# 45

As my best friend, my lover, and my archaeologist, Janice decided to bury me alive in sand at Topsail Beach. We were going down there for the weekend anyway. After hearing me recount the long and unhappy talk I'd had at the Same Place with Christopher, Janice said I was another cultural outsider about to be entombed by the prevailing cultural power, meaning journalism in general and Perrault in particular, so Janice envisioned for me a ritual burial in sand. I asked her if sand had some ancient significance. She said no, it just meant she wouldn't have to use a shovel. And so late on Saturday morning, about eleven o'clock, we formed our burial procession and left the motel in sandals and swimming suits, carrying with us

292

such vital burial implements as some towels, Coppertone suntan lotion, some M&Ms, a little Sony radio and tape player, a copy of *Crime and Punishment,* a notepad and pen for my final remarks in this transitory life, a paperback Bible, and a small cooler with devotional things in it, like some Michelob Dry and Royal Crown Cola.

Janice picked a spot in the dirty white sand, sand that was the color of dirty rice, right at the border of where the endless waves flattened out and grew quiet and tiny as they slid transparent over the sand and backed into the ocean again. There, she sat facing the ocean in the dark, moist sand, digging up big handsful of sand that she began shaping into a kind of mound.

"This is your sand pillow," she said as she formed it. "You need something to rest your head on."

"What for? The dead don't rest," I said.

She looked over at me and said, "Don't be morbid while I'm making your tomb."

"Yes, ma'am."

Once the sand pillow was finished, Janice started scooping out a little shallow area for my torso and hips and legs, making me realize we really were doing this. It was a grotesque, ritual joke symbolizing my vanishment and death. It unnerved me a little that Janice, who was both the priestess and the laborer for my burial, might still be hurt enough from my story that she'd find it strangely enjoyable to put me under sand and see no reason to stop.

She halted her tomb construction to open a bottle of Michelob Dry and take a big drink.

"Is it a primordial burial custom to drink beer when you're making a tomb?" I said.

She nodded her head and said, "Yes. The Egyptians often drank beer while they were making the great pyramids. That's why the construction took so long."

She wiped her hands on her thighs to get the sand off her hands, then searched through her bag for a religious tape to play during the ritual. We'd wanted to get Handel's *Messiah* but couldn't find it, so we settled on a tape she'd made with some Beatles songs. Putting the tape into the player, Janice stared at me solemnly and said, "Let the dirge begin."

She pushed the button and on came "Twist and Shout."

"That's a good dirge," I said, opening a can of Royal Crown Cola and lighting a cigarette as Janice resumed scooping out wet sand to assume the form of my declining form.

"Do you want to dance?" I said.

She smiled slightly and said, "You can't dance at a burial. It's disrespectful."

During the scooping, a couple of small crabs poked their heads from my tomb and ran away.

"I hope there aren't any more crabs down there," Janice said. "It wouldn't be a very dignified burial with crabs pinching you."

The digging was soon done to her satisfaction, and she said, "Okay. Lie down with your head on the sand pillow."

"I have to put on my burial shroud," I said.

"We don't have a shroud. Just put on your Cleveland Indians cap."

I did, saying, "This way, when archaeologists dig me up two hundred years from now, they'll know what tribe I'm from."

This was formally the burial. I lay myself down with my head propped up softly on the sand pillow, relaxing in the cool, damp sand as Janice knelt beside me holding two handsful of sand above my stomach and we looked at each other. We hadn't worked out a precise ritual.

"Man born of woman," Janice said, stopping there to look down at me for help. "I don't remember the complete sentence," she said.

"Man born of woman comes out of the uterus," I said.

"It doesn't sound biblical. I'll just try a different ceremony," she said, closing her eyes briefly, opening them, then saying, "Ashes to ashes, dust to dust."

"Janice. We don't have any ashes or dust."

"Well, I'll have to go back to the motel and get some."

"Just use the sand."

"I don't know any rituals with sand. I need to say some spiritual things. I can't just dump wet sand on you."

"Yes you can. This is a new ritual. Just dump wet sand on me and say 'There.'"

"There?" she said. "It's not very elegant or solemn."

"Being buried alive in sand isn't elegant."

"You're right," she said, moving her fingers apart to let sand spill onto my stomach. "There," she said, smiling.

Now that the burial had begun in earnest and I felt a little dizzy, wondering if Janice might eventually abandon the simple ritual and bury me forever, she moved a little faster, rhythmically scooping up sand and gently plopping it along my stomach and chest. It only took a few minutes for her to cover most of my torso, and now she hesitated.

"I'm ready to start down there," she said, holding some sand over that crucial organ between my legs. She patted me there and smiled.

"Do we have a special song for this part?" I said.

"You mean organ music? We didn't bring any," she said, covering the middle of me with sand and moving on quickly to my legs and feet. Gradually a smooth mound of sand rose above me nearly a foot at its highest point over my stomach. The sand was heavy and wet, making me feel trapped in the earth and, which was only true, helpless. Janice put her towel down near my head and sat next to me so her shadow blocked the sun from my face and we could look at each other. On the tape player, the Beatles were singing "Back In the USSR," and Janice took my paperback Bible from her bag.

"What do you want me to read?" she said.

"Read the whole Bible," I said. "It should only take four or five days."

She sipped some Michelob Dry and wiped some sweat from her nose.

"Just open it at random and read the first thing you see," I said.

She flipped open the Bible, squinted at the page and began reading aloud:

"And David said to Uriah, Go down to thy house, and wash thy feet. And Uriah departed out of the king's house, and there followed him a mess of meat from the king."

She stopped and looked at me. "A mess of meat?" she said. "That doesn't sound biblical. It sounds like Jethro, from the 'Beverly Hillbillies.'"

"Do it again," I said. "Flip some pages and read something else. It's all very spiritual."

She did it, and read this:

"When a man hath taken a new wife, he shall not go out to war, neither shall he be charged with any business: but he shall be free at home one year, and shall cheer up his wife which he hath taken."

"That's nice," I said.

"Yes," Janice said, sipping some beer and flipping through the pages again. "But I'm not doing it at random anymore. I'm going to read that part in Ecclesiastes you picked out last night."

I watched her look through the pages until she finally stopped.

"Here it is," she said, staring down at me in her shadow as she read the passage:

> "Then I looked on all the works that my hands had wrought, and on the labor that I had labored to do: and behold, all was vanity and vexation of spirit, and there was no profit under the sun."

"Yes," I said. "All was vanity and vexation of spirit, and I hurt you, without excuse or understanding. And I alienated Perrault, that Philistine fuckhead whose ignorance and narrowness is the law. And though I walk through the valley of death, the ravine of despair, the ditch of grief, the culvert of psychological disorders, I will fear no evil, because I'm too stupid. You can bury me now."

Janice put her hand on my cheek. "You *are* buried," she said.

"Put on your black veil now and mourn for me."

"Oh. That's right," she said, then reached into her bag and pulled out a little black hat with a black veil on it. She smiled as she put it on, and said "I'm mourning, now. Do I look nice?"

"You're pretty. I'm glad I love you."

She touched my cheek again, rubbing her fingertips along my skin. "Now that you're buried, now that you're immobile and helpless, what do you think you should do? Sink or sink?"

"It's not a very good choice. I don't believe in failure, no matter how many times I do it."

She took the veil off and tossed it into the sand behind her as she stared at me and moved her face closer to mine. I wanted to hold her, but I couldn't move.

"Are you going to kiss me?" I said.

"No. I'm going to suck your brains out through your ears," she said quietly, laughing a little bit with her lips on mine.